The Check Out

A Novel by

Richard A Lester

Richard A Lester
http://www.richardalester.com
mail@richardalester.com

Published by 360 Digital Books.
Electronic Book published by Amazon.com

Cover Designed by Damian Browning.
http://www.thegravy.co.uk/

First Edition 2013

For Mom, Dad, April, Ayden, Elwyn, and Bryson.

But, especially for Kat.

Acknowledgements

I have to admit that I had no intention of writing a novel when I began working a grocery store job three years ago. Over time, I became struck with the mundane qualities of the day to day routines, and frequently day dreamed events to make things more interesting. So used to writing screenplays that would never go before cameras, I decided to commit these flights of fancy to page. I had assumed that I, alone, would be responsible for the material and its distribution. I was completely mistaken. If not for the following people, you would not be reading this right now.

First, and foremost, I have to thank Katherine Moore for pushing me to write the damn thing in the first place. A brilliant writer, she provided me with an avenue for my ideas that I would never have discovered for myself. She also provided editorial insight, despite a frantic schedule and her own commitments.

Second, I must thank Lucy Gillespie for painstakingly going through the manuscript to fix grammatical errors and to tighten loose ends. There aren't many people that would disrupt their wedding planning to do this!

Thank you to Sam Bahre, John Shaw, and all the guys that helped me film the trailer. Not only is it a great tool to push the book, but it also allowed me to feel closer to my first love of movies.

A huge thanks to Damian Browning for designing the cover. This is truly a work of art!

Finally, I would like to thank each and every person reading this book. After working on this project (off and on) for over two years, it's a dream come true to have it in your hands. I hope you enjoy reading it as much as I enjoyed writing it.

I hope that you enjoy this book, and would appreciate your honest feedback. You can leave comments at my web site, send me an email, or leave reviews at Amazon.com. I also have a mailing list that you can subscribe to. I will occasionally be sending out updates, as well as free stories and other goodies. I hope you join.

Thank you,
Richard A Lester

Official Site: http://www.richardalester.com

Email: mail@richardalester.com

Amazon: http://amazon.com/author/rlester

The Check Out

Prologue

A cloud of smoke billowed from Arnold Knight's mouth and out the window of the moving WTMC news van. He took another drag and threw the spent butt into the street. The energy pills he had bought at the gas station down the road were just beginning to kick in. After twitching in his seat for a moment, Knight reached into his pocket and pulled out another cigarette. Once again, he held the pack absently to the driver (who also happened to be the cameraman) and once again, the driver shook his head.

"Jesus Christ." Knight spit the words, along with saliva, into the hot air outside. "What the fuck did we do to deserve this assignment?"

Arnold Knight had been an anchorman at WTMC for fifteen years. During his time with the station, he had covered political scandals, murders, robberies, high profile court cases, and even a few kidnappings. Unfortunately, a DUI arrest followed by a nasty divorce, in which highly embarrassing personal details had been divulged, had knocked Knight out of favor with the public. These days, he was lucky to cover a dog show or street renaming. In fact, he was more likely to be found at the Platinum Pony drinking tequila shots and harassing dancers than at City Hall interviewing the mayor.

He received his current assignment after returning to the station from covering a fundraising event for the local high school. Today, he would have the honor of documenting a cash giveaway at a failing supermarket in a bad part of town. The story would run once during the early broadcast, near the end…and only if they were running under time.

As he took another drag, Knight flipped the visor down and the mirror-cover up. His white hair, slicked back with gel, shone brightly in the early morning light. Knight tilted the visor and caught a glimpse of his eyes; they were bloodshot and weighed down by heavy bags. Though he was only fifty-four, his recent lifestyle choices had aged him twenty years. He flipped the second butt out of the window and reached behind him for his makeup kit. It would take nearly a pound of powder to make his face TV worthy.

"I don't know how in the hell I'm gonna get this shit to stick to my face," Knight complained as he dabbed the applicator. "It's gotta be a hundred fucking degrees out here already."

He turned to elicit an agreement from the driver. All he got was a noncommittal grunt. Knight returned to his kit and compact mirror.

"You'd think after thirty fucking years of doing the weather that Charlie could get something right occasionally." Knight rubbed base under his eyes. "I thought he said it was supposed to rain or something today."

"I think that was last week." The driver's tone struck Arnold's ego.

Knight turned to face the driver seat.

"How old are you, son?"

"Twenty."

"And how long have you worked for the station?" Knight attempted to keep his anger in check.

"Six months."

"Well, then, son..." Knight wound himself up for another tirade against the injustices of getting old and being divorced. He usually reserved his speech for last call at the local hole in the wall. In fact, he had just given a brilliant recitation four hours ago. The flashing red and blue lights stopped him mid-sentence.

"What the fuck is going on here?" Knight stared through the windshield. His eyes widened and he dropped the powder-covered sponge to the floorboard.

"Isn't that the store that we're supposed to cover?" The driver's voice raised several octaves.

The entrance to the MegaSaver was bathed in the strobing lights of police cars, fire trucks, and ambulances. Yellow tape was being strung around the building to prevent the crowd of onlookers from interfering with the crime scene. From across the street, Knight could see a sheet-covered body being wheeled out of the supermarket and rolled into the back of a waiting ambulance.

"Drive! NOW!" Knight slammed his hand against the dashboard several times, stirring his driver into action. Before the van came to a complete halt in the lot, Knight jumped from the passenger seat.

"Get back, get back!" A police officer stretched his arms wide to block the reporter's charge.

"Arnold Knight: WTMC!" The reporter's voice boomed with excitement and authority. The young cameraman stumbled into him, attempting to load a tape into the camera, power it on, and focus it all at the same time.

"I don't care who you are, you can't cross the tape." The policeman shook his head and took a step forward.

Suddenly, a wild cry came from the entrance of the store. The reporter jerked his head around towards the sound. Knight watched as police led a weeping man out of the grocery store and off to the side. With another moan of anguish, the man ripped his shirt open and threw it onto the concrete. As Knight stared in amazement, the hairless man curled into a ball and rocked on the pavement. He couldn't quite make out the man's crazed words, but he thought he heard something about karma and gross profits.

"You better be taping this shit, kid." Knight stared at the naked man now contorting himself into various yoga positions.

"Mr. Knight,' the cameraman pressed a Bluetooth set in his ear, "the station wants us to go live in five."

Knight whipped his head around to face the camera. His eyes instantly sharpened; the bags under them lifted. Knight's posture straightened and he took command over the situation. It even appeared that the blotches of uneven makeup vanished in the bright light of the reporter's rediscovered confidence.

The young man steadied the camera on his shoulder and counted down the seconds with his fingers. Despite the chaos that was unfolding behind him, and the lack of official information to report, Arnold Knight cleared his throat and prepared to relaunch his career.

Chapter 1

The air was hot and sticky as the mid-July sun scorched the sky. Once-manicured lawns had become brittle and wilted as sprinklers fought in vain against the festering heat. The sidewalks had become giant griddles, encompassing the dying grass like electric fences. Mounds of exposed flesh bounced up and down, rippling out from underneath thrift store T-shirts and undersized cut-off shorts. The faint smell of body odor and discount cigarettes lingered in the air and clung to anyone who waddled through it on their way into the MegaSaver entrance.

The grocery store stood in the middle of a neighborhood long forgotten by anyone who could afford to. The building, with its flaking paint and leaky roof, was surrounded by empty parking lots and vandalized gas stations. Pot holes littered the streets leading to the store. The parking lot was pocked with trash and missing concrete.

Larry Prescott eyed the herd of customers wandering aimlessly, stalking them with his lion eyes. Behind his blind-drawn windows, Larry studied the position of each customer, cart, and carry-out boy, waiting for his moment to pounce. Would a box of chicken wings fall out of a basket? Would an employee duck behind a car for an unscheduled smoke break? Larry wished he could smell the draw of blood through the glass window of his air conditioned office.

At five feet, seven inches, most people would not consider Larry Prescott tall. In fact, many who did not know him would say he was short. Those who worked for him, however, knew the true power behind his small frame. He was a beast at heart; a man to be feared and respected. Though wisps of hair were plastered over his growing bald spot, most would swear to the thick mane surrounding his head. He was king of his domain; master over all that he surveyed. He protected his own, and ripped his enemies to shreds. He was powerful and terrifying, yet commanded love and admiration from those beneath him.

A soft knock startled him from his stalk, and Larry turned bitterly towards the office door.

"Come in," Larry's voice roared. There was a pause. His eyes bore through the wood in disgust. He cleared his throat and tried again. "Come in."

The door opened to reveal the nervous smile of a twenty-five year old employee named John Turner. He stood cautiously as the door squeaked open. A bead of sweat dripped down his forehead as he stared at his boss.

"I'm sorry, I guess I didn't hear you…" John's words trailed off.

Larry stared at him for a moment, unable to believe that his voice had not carried through the door and down the hall. He swallowed his anger and met John's eyes with his own.

"Well… what do you want?" Larry's voice barked more than bellowed.

John took a step inside the office. His hands shook slightly, and he grasped his baggy, denim pants to secure them.

"Oh, well," John swallowed hard, trying to find the words. "I've been thinking…"

A snort from Larry cut him short.

"Do I pay you to think, son?"

John looked down towards the concrete floor.

"Uh…no, sir. Not really…" he stammered.

"You're goddamned right I don't. I pay you to check in my produce and keep my freezers full of dead animals."

John licked his lips.

"Well, isn't that right?" Larry had cornered his prey with just a couple of sentences.

"Yes. Yes sir. You do." John's knees began to quiver.

"What's with all this thinking then?" Larry bent his back legs, preparing to pounce.

"Well, I was just thin….I mean, I believe that yesterday was my one year anniversary with the company, and I just wondered if maybe a raise…"

6

"A RAISE?" Larry's mouth was wet with spittle. "Do you know what a raise is, son?"

John opened his mouth to reply, but Larry continued.

"A raise is a reward for someone who does a good job. No, screw that, a fantastic job. A raise is something you give someone who works his ass off and makes things happen. Do you think you make things happen, John?"

A tear formed at the base of John's eye. Larry grinned, exposing a portion of his stained, crooked teeth.

"Yes, sir. I think I do make things happen."

"Not for the better!" Larry was enjoying the juicy soft meat of his lamb's throat. "Remember that pallet of pork chops that came in April? You remember what you made happen then? You made the fuckers spoil! That's what you made happen."

"No, sir. That's the way they came in…" John attempted a feeble protest.

"Then, " Larry continued without pause, "You let a whole shipment of hamburger patties get freezer burned."

"It was just two cases…" John's dying corpse flapped once more in Larry's jaws.

"And not just two weeks ago, you left a whole pallet of ribs out of the freezer and they completely thawed! I had poor Jose scrubbing the blood off the floor for a month afterwards. Hell, that's probably what put him in the hospital!" Larry's breath was hot and heavy.

"Jose? He was in a car wreck two days ago…" John took a step back only to bump into the office door that had mysteriously closed behind him.

"I'll tell you what, John." Larry's voice had suddenly calmed and almost invited him to have a seat.

John took a step forward towards the chair in front of him. He placed his hand on the back. Larry's stare rebuked him for such a brazen act of affability.

"I'm gonna make something happen for you, John," Larry stood protected behind his desk as he prepared his final blow. A small sliver of a smile curled his lips.

"Yes, sir?" John asked; his voice was hopeful and naïve.

"I'm gonna make you fucking unemployed!" Larry blustered.

"What?" John's voice cracked as the tear finally fell from his eye.

"You heard me, son. Take your raise and your thoughts and get the fuck out of my store!" Larry's volume challenged defiance.

John turned and accidentally hurled himself into the closed door. His face burned with pain and embarrassment; his eyes stung with tears and anger. His hand fumbled for the doorknob as Larry growled behind him. Eventually, the door flew open and John ran out, never to be heard from again.

Larry chuckled to himself. He wiped the blood from his lips and picked up the phone. He dialed a three digit number and hit the "Intercom" button. He was surprised, but not displeased, to find an erection bulging in his pants.

Chapter 2

Terrence Claybrook slowly opened his eyes and reached over to the nightstand. He slammed his hand down to stop the shrill buzz that had been piercing his dreams for the better part of an hour. The room was instantly silent and Terrence was grateful. He turned to check the time: 7:43 am. He sighed and laid his head back down on his damp pillow. Sweat glistened from his forehead and bare chest. The air conditioner in the bedroom was set at 68 degrees.

Terrence stared at the white bumps on the popcorn ceiling. He knew them well, having counted them night after night in vain attempts to bring sleep. Within the field of his vision, he knew exactly how many crumbs protruded from the ceiling. Over time, he had even outlined patterns of specks; going so far as to name each constellation.

When sleep did come to Terrence, it often brought visions of fear and isolation with it. As he stared at the ceiling this morning, he tried desperately to erase the images from his mind. He replayed scenes of laughter, birthdays and weddings in his head; any gleeful memory to supplant the ones that had crept in the night before. He had almost rid himself of dread when the bedroom door opened.

"Honey? Are you up?" an angelic voice wafted from the hallway and washed Terrence in peace.

He sat up and watched his wife walk into the room. Felicia was tall; well-figured. Her hair and makeup were already finished and she was dressed for work. She smiled at Terrence like an amused parent as she stepped inside.

"Didn't you hear your alarm? It's been going off forever."

"I'm sorry sweetheart," Terrence hoped his wan smile truly conveyed his apology. He knew he had probably kept her up all night with his tossing and turning.

9

"It's okay, dear. Did you get any sleep at all?" Felicia gently wiped the sweat from her husband's chest. Her hand stroked his stomach and brushed across the scar on his abdomen. Her light brown skin contrasted the dark ebony of his.

Terrence pulled the covers back and swung his feet around to the floor. He quickly jumped out of bed and headed towards the bathroom. His long legs carried him half the distance with one step.

"Yeah, I slept pretty well," he lied. He was glad she couldn't see his face through the bathroom door.

"Ok, I've gotta run to work, but I'll see you tonight, right?" Felicia raised her voice over the sound of running water.

"Yeah, I'll be home around 7," He yelled back. The warm water felt good on his skin; the soap washed away his doubts. By the time he stepped out of the shower, he was a new man.

Terrence opened the door and stepped out. His wife still sat on the bed, staring at his half naked body. The smile on her face was an invitation. Terrence smirked in return.

"I thought you had to go…" Terrence eyed Felicia with hunger and a building excitement.

"I decided I couldn't wait until 7." Felicia leaned back on the bed and unbuttoned her blouse.

Terrence grinned playfully as he dropped his towel and climbed into the bed. He removed his wife's clothes and he pressed his lips against hers. Her touch lulled any concerns he had for being late to his shift at the MegaSaver.

Chapter 3

The King Hotel was a run down dump surrounded by housing projects. It was old, brittle, and appeared to be in danger of collapse at any moment. The paint was chipping and the neon sign hadn't displayed the "I" and "E" for years. The sounds of gun fire and domestic disputes were commonplace, and the sight of blue flashing lights usually greeted anyone checking in after dark. Most of the customers were business men entertaining women of one sort or another. Hard drugs and bodily fluids were exchanged as frequently as lifted CD players and stolen cash. Most people were either ignorant of the hotel's existence or avoided it all together. But Roland Tillman wasn't most people.

Roland lay on top of the yellowed sheets that covered his twin size bed and flipped through an issue of *FUPA* magazine. A stream of smoke rose from the Marlboro Red that rested between his lips. His eyes were transfixed on the images of naked, overweight women in front of him; they both disgusted and entertained him. He was revolted by the women's bodies and the wretched acts they performed on themselves, yet he couldn't put the magazine down. Each turn of the page brought an appalled laugh and a moment's distraction.

Roland took a drag from his cigarette and dumped the ashes on the carpet, using an orange stain as a makeshift bull's-eye. A dry cough forced its way up through his throat as he placed the Red between his lips. Roland turned the page and rested his hand on his chest. He rubbed his peck, and briefly considered playing with himself, before finally throwing the disgusting magazine across the room.

His dusty brown hair was streaked with white strands. His face was wrinkled beyond his years; dark circles seemed to permanently frame his eyes. His body was still fit, a testament to his meager workouts, and infrequent meals. Tattoos covered much of his weathered skin; scars took care of the rest.

He sat up in bed and looked around at the filth-covered room. The furniture was old, scratched, and most of it wobbled. There was no television on the dresser; it had long ago been stolen and pawned for a quick fix. The walls had perhaps once been white, but were now the color of cigarette smoke and age. There was even a dash of blood in a corner. Even so, it wasn't the worst place Roland had ever stayed at. He rose to take a piss.

The bathroom floor was sticky, and the sink dripped like an open wound. The shower was in slightly better shape, having been cleaned by Roland the first night he checked in. He could live in filth if he had too, but he was determined to wash it off himself occasionally. He stepped over to a pair of underwear that had arrived before him and unzipped his fly.

Roland sighed and opened his mouth enough for his spent cigarette to fall into the toilet. He targeted the butt with a stream of urine in a childish reminder of Asteroids, or some other game he played in his teens. He coughed once more, aimed, and rocketed phlegm towards the besieged cigarette. How the fuck had he ended up here?

He had spent years dreaming about this life. He had lain awake night after night imagining a future and all of the luxury it would bring. He thought about the house he would own, or the car he would drive. He pictured the woman that he would wake up next to every morning, or the kids he would pick up from school every afternoon. He thought about the job he might have, and the friends he might barbecue with on weekends. This was about the farthest thing from those dreams he could have envisioned. The years of running had been nearly as bad as the years inside.

Roland zipped his pants and flushed the toilet. The water continued to rise until it overran the bowl. He took a step back from the piss covered floor.

"Fuck this," he spat as he stormed out of the bathroom. Maybe he was broke, but he didn't have to put up with a shit hole like this. There was bound to be another hotel somewhere that took cash and didn't ask questions.

Roland grabbed a shirt from the black bag underneath the rickety bed. He lifted the pillow he had rested his head on and grabbed the .44 magnum from its hiding place. He tucked the gun into his pants at the small of his back, and pulled down his long sleeves to cover the snake tattoo on his wrist. He lit another cigarette and snuck a peek through the window blinds. He scanned the parking lot around him; his eyes eventually fixed on a 1994 Ford Taurus on the far end of the lot. He opened the door softly and quickly made his way toward the car.

Instantly, he noticed the bored-out locks on the driver side door and smiled. The one good thing about this neighborhood was the ease with which he could steal a car. People around here were so used to their cars being broken into or vandalized that they rarely got them repaired afterwards. In fact, most had even stopped reporting the thefts, as they never had insurance, and the police hardly ever recovered the vehicles.

Roland climbed into the car and ducked down. The starter wires were already exposed and held together by electrical tape. They hung below the steering column in resigned acceptance. The car started easily and Roland pulled out of the parking lot without alarm. He slowly made his way around the corner, passing a police car on the way. He held the speed limit for several blocks, arousing no suspicion.

As Roland drove down Washington, he began scanning for a new dump to spend the night in. He had enough money to get him through the next week or so. As he pondered his next move, Roland took notice of the MegaSaver on his right.

"Easy money," he thought. He circled the lot twice and pulled back into the street.

Chapter 4

Brad was awake, but unable to see. He was surrounded by darkness, and was only mildly aware of his own body. His thoughts were hazy and unfocused. Somewhere, in the distance, he thought he heard a steady rumble. A sliver of light began to break through the black fog, and Brad realized he was opening his eyes. For a moment, he couldn't discern exactly what he was looking at. A white, sweaty blob covered his entire view.

He attempted to raise his arm but was met with stiff dissent. His muscles were locked into position and defied any order to loosen. A cramp shot up his foot the moment he tried to lift his leg. Wait.....was he lying on the floor?

As he contemplated his next move, he saw something that disturbed him. There, floating in front of the strange white blob, were small wafts of steam. No... not steam. They looked familiar, but he just couldn't place them. Were they coming from his mouth? Holy shit. It was his breath.

Sensation began to stir in Brad's skin and he finally realized that he was shivering. He felt his face pressed against something hard, something concrete. His finger finally shifted without causing him pain. It was soon followed by the others, and eventually by his hand and arm. He pushed against the ground and felt himself rise.

A sudden wave of nausea flooded his stomach and caused his head to spin. He closed his eyes in a futile attempt to prevent the eruption from his mouth. As the sickness subsided, his vision steadied once more. He rubbed his face with cold hands and looked back down towards his feet. Next to the puddle of vomit sat the white blob now acutely defined: a gallon of 2% milk.

Brad looked around the room and felt a familiar disappointment. He put his left foot in front of the right, balancing himself against the wall. When he opened the door, he finally felt warm air against his skin and his muscles rejoiced.

"That is the last fucking time I ever do this shit," Brad chided himself. He reached into his pocket and pulled out three small orange tablets. Wearily, he made his way towards the trash can and held his hand above it. He wasn't sure if it was muscle stiffness or something else, but he couldn't force his fingers to open. As he stared at his hand, he debated with a voice in the back of his mind. Before he knew it, his hand had returned to his pocket.

Brad kicked the trash can in anger and discouragement. He realized that today would not be the day he went straight. He decided to clean himself up in the bathroom and get back to work. His strength gradually returned to him with each step. He closed the cooler door, and walked out to the sales floor of the MegaSaver.

Chapter 5

The flow of smooth jazz overhead was shattered by the booming voice from the Megasaver's intercom. It was gruff, proud, and threatening. All around the store, employees stopped and raised their heads like obedient dogs. They abandoned customers and tasks alike as they awaited their master's command. Everyone that is, except for Maxine Watkins.

Maxine walked toward her cash registers with deliberate ease and stared straight ahead. She nodded and said hello to everyone that she passed, and even stopped a few times to give directions. She showed absolutely no sign of acknowledgement when she heard her name ring from the overhead speakers. She smiled and kept walking at her own pace, refusing to be disturbed by the little man above her.

Maxine stood at five feet two inches, about the same size as the chip on her shoulder. Her curly, dark hair was pulled back, and she peered out at the world through large, dark lenses in frames that were twenty years old. She found no reason to update her style of dress, nor had the money to do so. In the five years she had worked at the MegaSaver, she had amassed just enough money for a small apartment a few miles away, a used Pontiac Grand Prix that barely got her back and forth to work, and the paperwork that finalized her divorce. Though it wasn't a lot, and she wanted better, she was proud of what she had, and protected it fiercely.

"Miss Maxine!" a short, chubby woman in a MegaSaver polo shirt exclaimed as she trotted up to her supervisor. "Mr. Larry just paged you! Didn't you hear?"

Maxine huffed with indifference and walked up to her nest at the customer service desk. Her eyes scanned the counter as she mentally took inventory of her clipboards, staplers, tape dispensers, paperwork, and various other items.

"Miss Maxine!" the chubby cashier repeated with panic, as if Maxine had missed it the first time.

"Yeah, I heard him." Maxine idly replied as she began rubbing cocoa butter lotion over her dark skin. She massaged her elbows and arms until her skin gleamed in the fluorescent light.

The chubby girl's breath grew more forced as she stared at Maxine, waiting for something to happen. Maxine continued kneading herself, purposefully ignoring the office above where she could feel Larry's eyes blazing towards her. A wry smile crossed her face as she set the lotion down, only to pick up a pencil, and begin writing something unnecessary on a sheet of paper.

"But Miss Maxine!" the chubby girl protested.

Maxine lowered her pencil and turned towards the chubby girl.

"Listen, child. If you jump just one time when a white man tells you to, he will own you the rest of your life. You understand that?" Maxine's voice held more anger than she meant for it to.

The chubby girl took a shocked step backwards.

"But, I'm white…" she stammered.

"Hmm," Maxine said as she resumed her needless scribble. "I guess that's your problem, sweetheart."

Chapter 6

Larry sat fuming in his office. He cursed to himself as Maxine leisurely walked over to the phone, stopping to talk to customers and cashiers on her way. It had been a full minute since he paged her to call his office, and he sat waiting as his blood pumped harder. Anyone else in the store would have sprinted; they would have nearly killed themselves to fulfill his desires. Maxine, however, openly defied his authority.

Perhaps, he thought, it had been his own fault. He had given her so much freedom over the past five years that, maybe, she felt immune to his influence. She was always the one who trained the cashiers. She handled the cart attendants when they were slacking or making lewd jokes in front of customers. Hell, she's the one that actually knew all their names. Maybe it was time to put her in her place.

The phone in Larry's office finally rang, and he snatched up the receiver with ferocity.

"Yes?!" Larry growled.

"This is Maxie. Did you need something?" Her slow, deliberately sugary southern accent had disarmed and emasculated him. It was clear she was in control.

"Come up to my office a minute," Larry slammed the receiver down before she could fire another shot.

"Just who in the hell do she think she is? Did *I* need something?" Larry's feet fell heavy against the floor as he began to pace.

"Did I *need* something? I don't **need** anything!" Larry pictured himself the wounded animal in danger of being overtaken by predators and scoffed. He took a deep breath and expanded his chest. He was king of this domain; she was a lowly employee. He was the one that made the tough decisions. He signed the paychecks every week….well, the time sheets anyway. He had the authority to hire and the power to fire. Just five minutes ago he had run the piss-poor freezer manager out the door with his piss-poor tail between his piss-poor legs.

Larry's blood began to pump harder again. He felt the movement in his pants and smirked to himself. Maybe he should go home for lunch. He could pop by the house for a quickie; a celebration in the sack. God, how long had it been? Too long.

He glanced over at the window and saw Maxie talking to a cashier. At first look, it seemed that Maxie was reading the other woman the riot act. Upon closer inspection, Larry discerned that she was just wasting time.

Larry turned back toward his office and his dirty thoughts. He imagined taking his wife by the back of the neck and kissing her down the length of her body. He would undress her from behind, working his way down to the small of her back. Next, he would turn her to face him, her breasts exposed and perky. After licking each nipple, he would move his hand down to her legs and feel her reaction. They would ravish each other, tearing the bed apart with passion and fire.

Larry stood in his office, fully erect and ready for action. The pressure in him had built to a critical level and he felt he might explode without a release. As he walked over to the phone, he noticed Maxine still chatting with the cashier. He decided to call her back and tell her to forget it; he was heading home to fuck.

As he reached for the phone, Larry caught something in the corner of his eye. His hand stopped on the receiver and he turned towards the wall. There, staring back at him was a portrait of his wife; a "Glamour Shot" he had paid for last year. Suddenly, he felt his blood pressure weaken and his penis go limp.

Larry had met his wife, Cynthia, eleven years ago at a grocer's convention in Minneapolis. He, along with 100 other grocery store managers, had been flown to the City of Lakes by a consortium of vendors hoping to push their products to a more prominent spot on crowded shelves. The store managers were there to eat for free, and get drunk on the vendors' dime.

During one of the many cocktail socials held throughout the weekend, this particular one sponsored by Checkmate Cereal, Larry had struck up a conversation with a pretty blonde woman sitting next to him at the bar. He liked the way she laughed at his lame jokes. She told interesting stories and shared the secret of how she raised her gross profit 15% over a four month period. Over a few drinks, they compared employee horror stories, talked about their families, and told each other their dreams for the future. At the end of the night, the blonde woman excused herself to return to her room, and left her number in Larry's pocket. Larry awoke the next morning to find himself lying next to the night-audit girl from the front desk; at breakfast he found out her name was Cynthia.

A few weeks later, Cynthia had called with some startling news.

"How the fuck did you get this number?" Larry wretched into his office phone.

"From the information you gave us at check-in...." Cynthia whimpered on the other end.

"Oh. Well, what do you want?" Larry interrogated.

Cynthia burst into tears and began rambling hysterically. Most of the words ran together, or were obscured by her sobs. There was only one word Larry heard clearly; a word that would define the rest of his life: pregnant. Within three months, Cynthia had moved into Larry's house, and become his wife.

At first, Larry accepted it; he even enjoyed it. A new wife and child gained him a wealth of attention from his employees and peers alike. He was the talk of the store; he finally fit in with the other managers in the company. It seemed that people took him more seriously; had a new-found respect for him. Women even stopped to talk to him when he paraded the baby around the store or park.

Once the novelty had worn off, however, Larry began to find the situation unbearable. He was constantly being woken up in the middle of the night by his screaming child. He was showing up late to work, and could barely focus on his

P&L reports. His wife was demanding more and more of his time; insisting that he come directly home from work instead of hitting up the local happy hours.

The regular sex, the one thing that kept Larry interested in the marriage, had even dried up. At first, Cynthia tried to win Larry's affections over with her body. She had never been the most beautiful of women, but she had always dressed nicely, and kept any blemishes hidden with makeup. She spent hundreds on sexy outfits and lingerie. She watched pornography and took notes. She tried every known position and moaned words that had once been against her religion.

Larry appreciated all of the pains that she had taken, and complimented her on them. He made sure to mention which lotions he liked, and which toys he found pleasurable. He paid attention to her body and often gave her grooming tips. When they had first moved in together, their sex had been constant and sensual.

After the kid came, however, things changed. Cynthia never lost the baby weight; in fact, Larry had noticed that she had continued to gain. She seemed bored, tired; uninterested in any advance he made. Her hair was constantly pulled into a ponytail, and her face was never made up. She had let her personal grooming go as well. Her legs were usually prickly, and there was a pencil thin moustache forming above her lips. There had once been a time when Larry lusted after his wife's figure, but now it was like fucking Bigfoot.

Larry's hand left the phone as he reconsidered his afternoon romp. By now, he was sweating and his bulge was becoming uncomfortable. He considered taking things into his own hands, but couldn't figure out just where to do it. There were too many windows in his office. (He shuddered at the thought of his employees watching him stroke himself high above them.) The bathrooms were downstairs and opened to the public. All it would take was some asshole bringing their kid in to change a diaper, and he would end up on some FBI list for the rest of his life.

21

As Larry mentally checked off a list of places to masturbate, there was a knock at his door. Out of habit, he yelled for the person knocking to enter.

Maxine opened the door and took a laggard step inside. "Yes?" she said lazily.

Larry raised his eyes to meet hers and stared deeply. His hopes raised and his voice lightened.

"Maxie! Let's go to lunch."

Chapter 7

Leonard Best sat on the bus stop bench and looked anxiously at his watch. The small awning provided little shelter against the searing heat, but it was the best that was available. He dabbed at his face with an old handkerchief and sighed. His eyes wandered, taking in the scenery around him. Although he had walked up and down this street a hundred times, Leonard hadn't really stopped to look at it in years. He could barely even recognize this as the street he had moved to over forty years ago.

Leonard's father, one of the first African American soldiers allowed to fight in WWII, had returned to the United States a changed man. The young, vibrant twenty-year-old mechanic had returned a broken, quiet casualty. His first meeting with his newly born son had been awkward and surreal. The hands that had caressed Leonard's mother had been replaced by blunt pieces of metal that could barely grasp a cigar or bottle of whiskey. Leonard's father had been unable to hold him for the first fifteen years of his life. For the next ten years, he had simply been unwilling. Leonard had been working at a grocery store, and on his own for three years, when he was told of his father's suicide. Though they hadn't spoken since their last fight, the news had hurt him in ways he couldn't have imagined. Luckily, Leonard had a new bride to offer consolation, and a child of his own to plan a future for.

Leonard had met Gladys on a hot summer day, not unlike the one he was now suffering through, in 1961. She and her father had been regular customers of the store he stocked groceries at, but Leonard couldn't bring himself to talk to her. Each time she and her father would come in, he would make up some excuse to go to the back of the store, or to another aisle; anywhere he could watch her from a safe distance. He laughed to himself, as he remembered his first thoughts about Gladys: "Her body is amazing." He would have liked it to have been more romantic, but his seventeen-year-old hormones had clouded the more evolved parts of his brain. He found out, many years later, that she had much the same thought about him then, too.

The day Leonard officially met Gladys, he had been sorting through the produce. Each morning he would come in and pull the spoiling apples and oranges from the good ones. The bad ones went into a basket and were placed on the front counter for a quick sale. Leonard was picking through the strawberries and hadn't noticed the customers behind him. He turned to walk to the bananas, bumping his basket full of over-ripe strawberries into Gladys's chest. The basket hit the floor, spewing fruit to the ground.

For a moment, Leonard stared into Gladys's shocked face. His hand had brushed against her breast, though accidentally. He stood in silence, fearing her scream and her father's vengeance. The blood drained from his face as he envisioned her father's hands wrapping around his throat and pummeling his body.

"Ma'am, I am so sorry." The words escaped without his consent.

Laughter burst from Gladys's mouth as she made no effort to hide her amusement. Her bright smile immediately put Leonard's mind at ease.

"Ma'am? Don't you know we're the same age?" Gladys continued to chuckle at the situation.

Leonard's face contorted in confusion for a brief second before his lips broke apart into a wide grin.

"Really?" He asked. "And how do you know how old I am?"

This time, Gladys blushed and coyly looked down at her feet.

"Well, I guess I must have heard from somewhere…" she smirked.

Leonard's smile broadened and he bent to pick up the mess at his feet. Gladys leaned over to help him, revealing a hint of cleavage. He struggled to keep his eyes on the fallen fruit.

"Oh, I can get this. It's my job…" Leonard attempted small talk.

"I don't mind." Gladys reached for the piece lying closest to his foot. She raised it up slowly and eyed it before handing it back to him.

"Well," He admired the strawberry, "it looks like you found a good one."

Gladys stared into Leonard's eyes for a moment.

"Yes, I believe I have."

Leonard and Gladys began seeing each other the next night. Movies, dances, walks in the park; they were inseparable for months. He saved every cent of his tip money, which wasn't much, to buy her a ring. When he could finally afford it, he proposed and she immediately said yes. Within weeks, they were married and moving into a small apartment on the street that Leonard now stared at.

Over the course of forty years, Gladys and Leonard had made a home for themselves and their three children. Leonard worked his way up in the grocery store and eventually bought it from the original owner. The store was small and it was gradually replaced by supermarkets and Wal-Marts that sprouted up around the city. Although it had provided enough income to raise their children, it never allowed them to move to the large house that Leonard wanted to offer his family.

Leonard and Gladys finally decided to close their store in the early nineties. It was a decision that had caused them as much grief as relief. They had made the walls of that store their home for so many years that they felt lost without it. Gladys's health, however, had made running the store more difficult with each passing year. Leonard was happy to finally have time to devote to her care and companionship. For the next ten years, they lived together in isolated bliss. Their children had grown and moved away, keeping infrequent contact as they became wrapped up in their own lives. He and Gladys spent most of their time playing board games and reminiscing about the "good old days." They took comfort in each other's company, and fell in love all over again.

Leonard looked down at his watch. The bus should be arriving at any moment, he thought. The sun was beginning to get to him. His face was moist, and his back was beginning to stiffen against the bench. A drop of sweat fell onto his neatly pressed, white dress shirt and he quickly tried to rub it away.

Leonard stood slowly to remove his suit jacket; attempting to ward off another errant bead of perspiration. He brushed pieces of fuzz from the sleeve, and picked a stray leaf from the back. He turned the jacket to face him and his breath caught. This was the first time he had worn this suit in three years. The first time since Gladys had died. Leonard sat down and attempted to swallow the catch in his throat.

Gladys had been diagnosed with lung cancer in early 2008. He remembered being absolutely dumbfounded by the test results. They had both begun to succumb to the inconveniences of aging: the swollen joints, arthritic pains, and occasional forgetfulness. Those problems, he was resigned to accept. Cancer, though, he could have never prepared himself for.

In the first few months, they fought against it. They hit the cancer with radiation and chemotherapy. Gladys lost her hair, her weight, and part of her dignity. Leonard always noted, however, that she never lost her smile. She faced each setback with strength and resolve, though, ultimately, she could not overcome her disease. After it was clear that nothing was helping, Gladys discontinued all treatment and decided to live out her final days with her husband at home.

At first, the children had provided immense support. They traveled from all over the country to be with their dying mother and to help their grieving father. They cooked meals and cleaned the apartment. They even helped with the growing hospital bills. When the inevitable day came, Leonard's children dutifully handled the funeral arrangements and softened the pain as much as they could. But after a few days, their lives beckoned them back to their respective parts of the country and Leonard was left alone.

He found it difficult to live in the apartment without Gladys. One of his sons offered to move him to Chicago to live in a guest bedroom. He thought about the move, but felt too old to start over in a new city. His daughter suggested a nursing home; an idea he scoffed at. This had been his home for forty years, and he eventually decided that it would be his home for the rest of his life. There were too many memories, and too much history, to simply move on.

Leonard was wiping tears away from his eyes before he noticed that he had been crying. He looked nervously around him to see if anyone had noticed. There was no one else at the bus stop with him, and the young, shirtless teenage boys that passed by never gave him a second glance. For once, Leonard was grateful to be invisible.

As the bus finally rounded the corner, he stood and put his jacket back on. He pressed his shirt with his hands to remove any wrinkles. He steadied his emotions and focused himself on the task at hand. As the bus door opened, Leonard climbed the step and headed towards the MegaSaver for his interview.

The warm California air became a cool breeze when it met the water droplets across Michael Standland's bare chest. He shuddered for a split second before regaining control of his nervous impulses and eradicating all thought from his mind. He exhaled, and began the fluid motions of his arms anew. He concentrated on his stance, the movements of his body, and ultimately, his place in the universe. As he touched the small of his back with his own foot, Michael contemplated the nature of man and the essence of his being. His train of thought was once again broken as he reached back to pull his leg closer to his body.

"Ooooo...." He thought. "Prickly." Michael ran his hand along his leg and felt the stumps of hair beginning to form. He frowned and wondered if he had time to shave before work. He realized the trespass of his thoughts, and took in a deep breath. He held the air in his lungs until he felt light headed; as he exhaled, his mind went blank once more.

Michael sat down, legs crossed, on his towel and stared at the swimming pool in front of him. Beyond the pool, a vast lawn spread out for several acres. Circles of well trimmed bushes and perfectly landscaped gardens bordered the yard. It had all been plotted and designed by Master Nu Aeg, the premiere fung-shui artist in the state.

Each morning, Michael awoke to a CD of natural bird noises and moved to the lawn for yoga and meditation. He had started the routine several years ago after a particularly troubling therapy session in which he had been referred to as a "man child" and told that he needed to "mature emotionally." The session ended with Michael throwing a lamp across the room and storming out. He never returned to therapy, but began researching his self help options. Eventually, he stumbled upon a book called "Age of the Soul: How to Maintain Youth With Yoga." It was written, of course, by the

Master Nu Aeg. Michael quickly finished the book, along with the Master's subsequent works, and completely redesigned his life.

Within a year, he had moved up from a lowly supervisory position to District Manager of Marketing for the Food Lot Corporation. His thoughts had focused, and he was routinely graced with bouts of creativity. Over the past several years he had instituted some of the most profitable advertising schemes in grocery retail. He had created the frequent shopper card, gas rewards, and even Buy One Get One Half Off. He was the man who put the "up to a dollar" in the "WE DOUBLE COUPONS! *up to a dollar" ad. Today, however, Michael was having trouble coming up with a plan for his latest endeavor.

He had recently been assigned a list of underperforming stores and was tasked with turning them around. At first, he had welcomed the project. He enjoyed reenacting the cycle of life with stores. They were born, they matured, and eventually they died. It was his job to rebirth them, and he had been very successful with most on the list. He had turned failing stores into huge profit centers with a few simple changes and gimmicky promotions. Most of the managers had welcomed him; his reputation provided him the red carpet. A few, however, were resistant to his ideas and subsequently had failed to implement them properly. As a result, Michael was now contacting his center of Zen for answers.

Finding no viable connection to Mother Gaia in his current position, Michael stood, removed the speedo swimsuit he had been wearing, and curled into a ball on his towel next to the swimming pool. As his hairless body curled upon itself, Michael buried his head amongst his entangled limbs. For a moment, he was unable to block out the noise around him. He heard every bird chirp, every car drive by, and every distant radio. He closed his eyes again, and finally willed away the world. The scorching sun above him began to sear his naked body, and sweat began to pour from his forehead. Michael's breath was reflected by his damp skin and only served to heat him further. He began to feel slightly dizzy, but did not change position.

Sufficiently detached from his surroundings, Michael opened his third eye and began to peer about the cosmos for answers to his dilemma. Visions began to fill his mind: he saw giant scissors and red banners, holiday displays and clearance sections. Eventually, visions of liquidation signs and empty shelves passed through his consciousness. Somewhere, however, in the distance, a shape began to form. Michael could not yet see the vision clearly; he reached his astral body's hand towards it.

His skin began to burn under the hot sun. His color went from healthy tan to bright red. Inside his imaginary womb, Michael's face dripped with sweat and he was in danger of heat stroke. Still, he reached towards his vision.

As the image drew nearer, its form became more defined. Though he was not aware of it consciously, Michael began to chant an "Ohm" of power to strengthen his psychic energy. With each repetition, the image drew nearer until....FINALLY! He saw it clear as day!

Michael's face broke fetal formation and he lunged for the pool's cool water. He emerged a new man; his red body was wet and his head was soaked. Primordial sounds erupted from his throat, and Michael's whole body shook. He slowly walked up the steps and out of the pool. He grabbed his towel and dried off. Still nude, he picked up his brief case and set it on his patio table. He opened the case and removed the financial documents within it.

Within the lines of numbers and figures, Michael could read a pattern. The Universe was sending him a message, and he was decoding it with ease. His whole plan lay within the documents and he quickly scribbled out his ideas for the ad campaign on the reverse side of the papers. He would start with the store in Orlando, then move to another in Pennsylvania. He would continue his trek throughout the country in strange patterns of zigs and zags, guided by destiny's hand, until he reached his final destination: the MegaSaver.

Chapter 9

Brad's hands trembled as he lifted a box of catfish fillets and put them into the freezer. He had spent ten minutes trying to steady them before finally giving up. His stomach rumbled with hunger, though he had no appetite.

Everything he looked at was still clouded and surrounded by a faint halo. People's faces were vague outlines; objects just impressions. Luckily, he knew the products and the employees well enough to wing his job. Customers, however, were another thing. He had already run from two of them, as he could barely make out what they were saying.

Brad's arm shook as he glanced at his watch. He jiggled his wrist in disbelief. How long had he been asleep in the cooler? He had only popped in there to feel the chill against his skin as warm intoxication took over his body. Surely, he couldn't have been asleep for as long as it appeared. Three hours? He wondered why Larry hadn't been on the war path looking for him by now.

Brad threw the last case of fish on the shelf and closed the freezer door. The smell of cooking food that wafted from the deli was upsetting his stomach and made him cough. He wondered if he should try to force something into his stomach; a wave of nausea made him think otherwise.

Sluggishly, Brad made his way over to the produce table and began straightening the bananas. It was a favorite task of his when he wanted to look busy without actually doing anything. He smiled and said hello as people passed. He addressed the blobs in red MegaSaver polos by their names; the others he referred to (sometimes incorrectly) as sir or ma'am. A few of the employees must have switched shifts. Brad didn't remember seeing them earlier...or did he? Once again, he vowed to throw the pills away.

"Brad, honey..." the chubby cashier placed her hand on his shoulder. "Are you alright?"

Brad looked down. He realized that he had absently piled all of the bananas on one side of the table, leaving a large hole in the other. He shook his head in disgust and smiled at the chubby cashier.

"Yeah, just trying to find the bad ones at the bottom." He hoped his words were clearer than he heard them.

The cashier stared at the pile of bananas and slowly nodded her head. She rubbed Brad's shoulder in a consoling manner.

"Ok." Her tone was doubtful. "But what are you doing here today?"

"What do you mean?"

"Well, you kinda disappeared yesterday, so we figured you went home sick." The concern in her voice was genuine. "And you're not scheduled today."

Brad dropped the bananas he was moving and looked at the woman. Her hair looked different than it did before he went into the cooler. He also noticed that she was wearing blue jeans instead of the khakis he had seen her in earlier. Oh god....how long had he been in there?

He took another look at his watch and his stomach turned in horror. He'd gone on break, and into the cooler, on Tuesday. His watch blindsided him with Wednesday's date.

"Yeah." Brad stammered for an excuse. "I started feeling better, and I wanted to finish this up, so I decided to pop by."

The cashier kept her eyes on his face. It was clear she wasn't buying it.

"I'll head out as soon as I get done with this." he tried once again.

Before she could say anything else, the chubby cashier was paged to the registers. A flash of fear went through her eyes and all else was quickly forgotten. Brad took a deep breath and dropped another bunch of bananas onto the table. How the hell could he have spent all night in the cooler? Didn't anyone go in there while he was passed out? Didn't the alarm go off?

Sweat began forming on his face again, and he decided it was best to leave. His stomach turned once more as he passed through the scent of cooking turnip greens. His eyes were constantly going in and out of focus; his feet were barely moving in a straight line.

The hot summer air knocked Brad back like a brick wall. His stomach rebelled, sending bile onto the sidewalk. His eyes scoured the parking lot, attempting to discern his van amongst the sea of vehicles surrounding him. Where the hell had he parked....yesterday? The realization taunted him once again.

Finally, on the other end of the lot, his bent up van shone like a beacon. Waves of heat hovered between him and his vehicle; Brad pictured himself crossing the concrete desert in his unstable condition and hoped he would make it. After stopping several times to vomit, he finally arrived at his destination. He pulled the driver's door open and climbed inside. A stream of slightly chilled air sputtered from the air conditioning vent as he turned the key. He leaned his seat back and closed his eyes. The sickness in his stomach settled and his brow began to dry. His hands shook less with each passing second; Brad could feel his body relax.

The sound of a honking horn caused him to jump. By now his head was pounding; Brad rubbed his face and reached up to put the van into gear. He stole a glance at his watch and did a double take; he'd lost another hour. He scolded himself and put his vehicle into reverse. He nervously pulled out of the parking lot and slowly made his way down the street.

Chapter 10

A bead of sweat lined Terrence's brow as he entered the MegaSaver. In just the few seconds it took to make it from his car to the front door, his shirt had begun to stick to him. The blast of cold air chilled him and caused his skin to rise. The clamor from the front registers made his head whip around.

Terrence stared in disbelief as two cashiers tried to fend off a line of customers five deep apiece. Phones were continuously ringing, and shopping carts littered the doorway. Across the store, by the deli, Terrence could see several employees gathered together, laughing. Anger seared his body, and he marched towards the customer service desk.

"What the hell is going on here?" Terrence's tone was more chiding than inquisitive. The flustered, chubby cashier grabbed the phone receiver and put the customer on hold.

"Larry and Maxine left for lunch about two hours ago, and things have just gone to hell!" the cashier's voice got more shrill with each word. "I can't get anyone up here to check or bag groceries to save my life!"

Terrence grabbed the phone and dialed a couple of buttons. The music overhead instantly stopped and his voice rang throughout the entire store.

"I NEED ALL CASHIERS AND BAGGERS UP FRONT IMMEDIATELY FOR CUSTOMER ASSISTANCE." Terrence's voice left no room for doubt or excuse. Within seconds, the employees had taken their positions and chaos was dissolved. Terrence nodded to himself with satisfaction.

"Now, what else is going on?" Terrence took charge. He would be damned if his day would start off like this.

The chubby cashier sorted through various papers on the desk and sputtered a list of issues that needed to be dealt with. Terrence listened and quickly fired off instructions. Satisfied that everything was back on course, he turned to make his way to the office. He could already feel a headache forming.

"OH!" the cashier ran up to catch Terrence. "I forgot something!"

"Yes?"

"There's a gentleman who's here for an interview. He's been waiting for, like, an hour." The cashier's eyes were big and apologetic. She handed Terrence an application.

Terrence nodded his head. "Alright, send him up."

The cashier smiled broadly and nodded her head. Terrence heard her thank God as she walked away.

As he climbed the stairs towards Larry's office, he tried to piece together the events of the day. He wondered what the hell was going on with Larry and Maxine. During his time as assistant manager, he had never known Larry to abandon his post as he had today.

Terrence opened the door to Larry's office and sat down behind the desk. He glanced through paperwork, trying to find clues to Larry's disappearance. A knock at the door brought his unsuccessful search to an end. He raised his eyes to see the chubby cashier standing next to an older black man.

"Mr. Claybrook, this is Mr. Best," the cashier cheerfully sang. "He's here for an interview."

Terrence smiled at the older man and wondered if they had met before. There was something familiar that he couldn't place.

"Mr. Best, I'm sorry to keep you waiting. It's been a hectic day," Terrence extended his hand towards Leonard.

Leonard Best smiled broadly and shook Terrence's hand.

"Please have a seat, sir." Terrence pulled out a chair for Leonard and took his own seat.

"Thank you," Leonard sat down nervously.

"I haven't had a chance to look over your application yet. Why don't you start by telling me a little bit about yourself and what your work history's been like," he put forth his most charming, apologetic tone.

"Well, my name is Leonard Best. I'm a widower, and I'm looking for some part-time work to bring in a little extra money," he shifted in his seat. "I've had a lot of grocery store experience in my life. I used to own a store a few years back."

Terrence leaned back in his chair and stared at Leonard.

"Oh yeah," Terrence began to recall something. "Where and when was that?"

"Well," Leonard smiled, "I owned the Third Street Market until about fifteen years ago."

Terrence stared into Leonard's eyes, but he was already a lifetime away. It had been almost twenty years ago, but Terrence realized that he had met Leonard before. His heart skipped a beat and his stomach flipped.

"I'm sorry, what was that?" he realized he hadn't heard the last few things Leonard had asked him.

Leonard stared at him for a second and cleared his throat.

"I asked if you were looking at other people for this position, too."

"Oh," Terrence's charm reengaged, "well, I don't really see a need to." Terrence stood and offered his hand. "Welcome to the MegaSaver family, Mr. Best."

Chapter 11

The hotel door burst open with a force more powerful than a gun shot. The stale mildewed air ignited and the energy of the room erupted. The walls began to spin; the light brightened. Larry slammed the door closed and pressed Maxine's body against it with his own. She pulled his mouth onto hers.

His lips pressed hard and electricity jumped from her skin to his. Larry felt Maxine's hand grasp his back and heard a subtle moan. He was unsure which one of them had made the sound.

Larry slipped his hand under Maxine's red polo work shirt and felt the soft cotton of her Wal-Mart brand bra. The stiff wire held her fleshy breasts in perfect shape. He massaged the tip of her nipple and felt it harden.

"Oh Larry..." Maxine's knees began to shiver and she felt faint. Her body alternately tensed and loosened as she felt Larry's hand run down the front of her khaki shorts. Her white cotton panties were moist with desire and her body tingled. Larry's finger slipped into her and Maxine bellowed with passion.

He couldn't believe what he was doing, or the fact that she was letting him do it. Perhaps it was his posture, or some sort of pheromone he was exuding, but she had picked up on his intentions immediately. On their walk to the car, they had nonchalantly discussed their various dining options in the area. They had even decided on trying out the new hot wings shop that had opened down the street. Once they got into the car, however, all thoughts of food were erased, and the kissing began.

For five minutes, they sat in Larry's assigned parking spot, devouring each other without a care in the world. They ignored the passing customers, and were unaware of any employees that happened to walk by. They were completely focused on each other and the physical needs they both desperately wanted to fulfill.

Larry pushed Maxine's pants-less body down on the bed. As she removed her top, he slid her underwear off. He pressed his tongue against slightly graying hair until he felt her clitoris. Maxine's body curled around him; her scream was deafening but her stout thighs protected his ears from permanent damage.

As Larry's tongue worked on his subordinate, he thought about the last time he had cheated. He had only been with one other woman since marrying his wife. Shortly after the birth of his child, Larry and Cynthia had fought bitterly about their lack of lovemaking and his late hours at work. She had started by simply asking if he could come home on time to watch the baby so she could run errands. Larry responded by transferring his sexual frustration to her. They yelled for thirty minutes and resolved nothing. The argument eventually ended with Larry storming out the front door and into the entrance of his favorite strip club: the Platinum Pony.

Larry had been coming to the club since he was old enough to get through the door. He knew most of the staff by name, and the dancers by alias. The bored-looking girl at the door went by the name Fuchsia, though by the look of her pale, pockmarked skin, it was obvious she hadn't seen daylight in years. Her stare was hollow, and the large sacks where her breasts should be hung awkwardly just above her rib cage. She passively waved Larry through and didn't even confiscate his coupon.

The words of his enraged wife still ringing in his ears, Larry took his usual seat at the bar and ordered a shot of whiskey. The bartender, Joe, was as much of an old friend as a bartender at a strip club could be and picked up on Larry's troubles quickly.

"Woman problem?" the bartender asked as he wiped down the counter.

"Fuckin' A, woman problem," Larry downed his shot and pushed the glass ahead for a refill.

Larry grimaced as the warm liquid burned a path down his throat, and coughed as his sinuses cleared. He eagerly took the next shot in his hand and downed it.

"I'll tell you what, Joe. Marrying that bitch was the worst fucking thing I have ever done." He held the third shot in his hand and stared at it as if divining his future.

"I should have told her to go fuck herself when she called that day. I should have never answered the goddamn phone."

The bartender nodded sympathetically as if a few memories of his own had crossed his mind.

"I should have told that bitch that she could either get the little fucker sucked out of her, or could raise it without me," the hate in Larry's words shocked him a little, and he glanced up to the bartender's eyes for any hint of judgment. "Am I wrong?"

Joe snorted a laugh and shook his head. "Man, hindsight's twenty/twenty, eh?"

Larry downed his shot and slammed the glass onto the bar. "No shit, my man. No shit."

By now the warm calm of Jack Daniels had begun to wash over Larry and he glanced around the room. Aside from himself, the bar was nearly desolate; most customers having decided to spend their Tuesday afternoon at work rather than at the club. Still, there were a few old men and desperate virgins sitting at the side of the stage, watching a woman named Cherry practice twirling the tassels at her breasts. A couple of topless dancers stood around the satellite stage, complaining about work and comparing cesarean scars.

Joe noticed Larry's eyes wandering around the room and leaned in. "Man, you know what you could use?" his voiced lowered for privacy.

"A fucking divorce?" Larry's voice was loud and booming. He laughed bitterly at the idea.

"No, man. Fuck that," Joe advised. "You know how much that could cost you? Half the house, half your money, not to mention the cost of all the actual court shit."

Larry frowned at the idea of giving anything else to the woman that sat at home crying. Hadn't he given her enough already?

"Man, what you need is a little….comfort." Joe smiled as Larry turned to face him. "You know what I mean?"

Larry pushed his glass towards the bartender and it was quickly filled. After a brief moment, Larry shook his head.

"I don't mind paying to see a little pussy, but I'm not gonna hire a whore. I can do better than that." Larry's ego clashed with his desire.

"Really?" the smile on Joe's face showed how many times he'd heard it before. Joe leaned in even closer to Larry and pointed behind him. "Better than that?"

The skepticism in Larry's face instantly melted when he turned to face the tall blonde woman sitting at a table across the room. She was beautiful and elegant, even in her break-away bikini top and thong. Her breasts were full and natural; her body was tight and smooth. The woman turned to meet Larry's eyes and she smiled warmly towards him. Larry couldn't believe he hadn't seen her when he arrived.

"Who is she?" His voice held wonderment and awe.

"She's new. Just started yesterday, " Joe began his pitch.

"Really? What's her name?" Larry hooked himself on the line.

"Man, who knows? Probably Porche or Candi or some bullshit you heard before. They don't tell us their real names," Joe lit up a cigarette and poured Larry another drink for free. "All I know for sure is, you'd be the first."

Joe pushed the drink towards Larry. After a moment, Larry grasped the glass and downed the shot. The bartender's close had been perfect.

"What do I have to do?" Larry asked.

"Just buy a dance. She'll take care of the rest." Joe nodded towards the woman. She walked towards the bar, smiling. Larry was hard by the time she placed her hand on his shoulder.

Without a word, the woman led Larry back to a private room. It was tiny, with only a small couch, but the time of day lent them enough privacy. The woman closed the curtain and removed her clothes.

The sex was enjoyable, though clinical and calculated. The woman's moves were choreographed for maximum pleasure in minimal time. In fifteen minutes, Larry had both a decent buzz and an orgasm. He had completely forgotten about his troubles as he resumed his seat at the bar. He ordered a cheap light beer and laughed with the bartender for another hour or so before finally returning home. He barely remembered signing his three hundred dollar tab.

Maxine's shrieks of joy returned Larry to the moment. She was holding him by the back of the head, as she writhed with pleasure. Finally, she brought his head up to meet her face and leaned into his ear.

"Oh, Larry," her southern drawl stretched the words out beyond their three syllables. "Fuck me."

Larry's erection exploded from his pants and he drove his penis deep inside Maxine. Her whole body shuddered and she yelled praises to God.

Larry pounded away and watched as Maxine's breasts flopped from side to side. Her body was not in perfect shape, like the woman's at the club, but her physical reactions more than made up for it. She was alive with passion; a force to be controlled.

He thought about her years of defiance and the way she had constantly bucked his authority at work. Perhaps they were real, or maybe they were subtle signs of flirtation. Maybe she had been using her audacity as a way of coming on to him. For all he knew, Maxine had been lusting after him for all five of the years she had worked at the MegaSaver.

A moan escaped from Larry's lips as he plunged deeper into Maxine. His white hand pinched her dark nipple and her brown skin jumped in excitement. Larry flipped Maxine over and entered her from behind. She clenched the off-white sheet below her and howled with delight.

Larry grabbed Maxine's shoulders and pelted her more intensely. He felt her body begin to quiver with orgasm; he thrust deeper and paused. Maxine reached back and grabbed Larry's pale white ass.

"Oh, don't stop, baby," she pleaded.

Larry leaned in to her ear and whispered "What do you want me to do?"

"Fuck me, baby. Fuck me!" the words dripped with desperation as Maxine hovered on the verge of sexual satisfaction.

Larry felt a surge of power over Maxine, a feeling that had eluded him the entire time he'd known her. He now held control over her body; he could either thrust her to climax, or leave her unfulfilled. His penis throbbed inside Maxine with excitement.

Larry thought of his great grandfather and the way he must have taken his house slaves again and again. The power…the control…He tasted a hint of dominance that had long ago been outlawed.

Larry's torso lunged forward causing Maxine's body to shake uncontrollably.

"Is that what you want?" Larry growled as he pulled Maxine's wet, curly hair.

"Yes, oh my God, yes!" Maxine's voice burst with joy.

Larry felt his own body tingle. His grip on Maxine tightened as he forced away the racial slur he felt compelled to yell. He was enraptured by his supremacy and sexual prowess. He had finally established command over his unruly employee, and discovered a new feeling of vigor in the process.

A roar burst from Larry's mouth as semen gushed from his cock. Both he and Maxine shook with ecstasy and then collapsed onto the bed. They silently stared at each other; surprised by both their actions and the satisfaction they got from them. Exhausted, the two were asleep within minutes. They lay naked, covered in sweat, their limbs forming a checkerboard pattern across the bed.

Maxine was the first to stir, steadying her wobbly legs as she raised herself from the bed. Larry watched her sagging figure as she made her way to the bathroom. He would have never guessed how much he would enjoy being with her until this moment. He was already feeling himself get hard again when he heard Maxine shriek.

"What's wrong?" Larry jumped up, throwing his pants on.

"The toilet backing up all over the floor!" Maxine shouted in disgust. "And somebody left their underwear in here!"

Chapter 12

Brad sat motionless for a few moments as comprehension caught up to his actions. His hand shook, his vision was hazy, and there was pain in his right leg. Blood dripped onto his shirt. A bright light surrounded him, and he could hear noise all around.

His hand wobbled down from the steering wheel as his vision cleared. His breath caught as he slowly realized what had happened. The cab of his van was crunched in towards him, and his knee was covered in blood. Through the fragments of his former windshield, Brad stared at the pole he didn't remember crashing into.

He pushed the seat with his hands, trying to wiggle out from the wreckage around him. After a moment, he had freed his injured leg and pulled the door handle. The door wouldn't budge.

"Fuck!" Brad rubbed the cut above his eye and wiped his face. Panic strangled him as he envisioned police descending upon his vehicle and hauling him off to jail.

With new resolve, he forced his bruised body to crawl across the seat towards the passenger door. As he turned that knob, the door wiggled slightly. He smiled faintly and took a deep breath. Brad lunged forward with all his strength causing the door to fly open. He fell face-first onto the smoldering concrete.

He lifted his head and spit. His front tooth splattered against the sidewalk. He turned towards the shattered carcass of his van. The sight horrified him; but not as much as the fact that he couldn't remember doing it.

"Oh my God!" Brad heard a woman's voice coming from the other side of the wreckage. A man's voice asked for a cell phone. Brad panicked as he heard the woman yell "Dial 911!"

Despite his injuries, Brad quickly fled down the suburban street and cut through an alleyway behind a convenience store. He stopped suddenly, adrenaline unable to compensate for the excruciating throb in his leg. He leaned against the wall and gently touched his knee. His hand jerked back as a wave of pain wrenched its way through his entire body.

Brad shook with fear and sorrow. What the hell was he going to do? Any minute, ambulances and police officers would pull up and ID his car. It wouldn't take them long to find him, either. They would either pick him up as he cowered in the alley or when he finally got home....to....his...WIFE.

"Oh, fuck, oh fuck!" Brad buckled over at the thought of his wife's rage. She would destroy the entire house by throwing shit at him. She may even beat him to death. Perhaps a few nights in jail wouldn't be so bad after all.

Brad's face clenched in agony as another shockwave ripped through his nervous system. If only he could stop hurting for a few minutes, he'd be able to figure something out.

Suddenly, a spark of hope shined in Brad's mind. He stuck his hand into his pocket and dug around. Where the hell where they? They've got to be in there somewhere....A ha! Brad pulled his hand out and stared at the pill resting in his palm. Where the fuck had the other two gone?

He decided it wasn't the time or place to attempt to solve such mysteries, and he swallowed the tablet. He closed his eyes and let the hot sun burn his face. Little by little, the light grew fainter and the pain receded. A few minutes after he had entered the alley, Brad hobbled out of it, feeling nothing. His pain, his fear; all had vanished. He turned the corner and entered the convenience store.

Brad shot past the foreign clerk before he had a chance to catch a glimpse of his mangled form. He grabbed the bathroom door handle and sighed with relief when it opened. He stepped in and quickly locked the door. He turned to the mirror and gasped.

45

He stared at the battered shape that used to be his face. By this point, his skin had already turned black and purple; the swelling had puffed the skin around his eyes. The cold water felt incredible against his face as he cleaned himself up. He removed his blood-splattered work shirt and threw it into the garbage can. His undershirt, though dirty, wouldn't get him noticed.

Brad exited the men's room in better shape than he had entered it, though there wasn't a huge improvement. He needed a way to cover the bruises and black eye, not to mention his bloody knee. After perusing the slim offerings of the Gas Mart, he finally settled on a pair of overly large sunglasses, a couple of bandanas to wrap around his leg, and a hat that boldly commanded: "Fuck Me, I'm Irish." He grabbed a screwdriver from the back aisle, and a tallboy can too. The clerk gave Brad an odd look, but said nothing as he purchased his disguise and exited the store.

Suitably incognito and anesthetized, Brad made his way back to the scene of the accident. He timidly approached the small group of people poking around the wreckage, and was thankful to see an ambulance pulling away from the scene with its lights off.

"What happened here?" Brad tested his disguise on one of the vultures hanging on the outskirts.

"Bad accident, man," the statement rang from the man's lips in an attempt to impress.

"Wow, really? They take the driver away in the ambulance?" Brad's breath stuck in his chest for a second.

"No, there was nobody here when they pulled up," the man sounded disappointed; "I figure someone ripped the van off and went for a joyride. Probably crashed this shit just for fun."

Brad's spirits lifted. "Is that what the police think?"

The man laughed and turned to face Brad. "Shit, man. It hasn't even been an hour yet. Those fuckers are still cruising donut shops or something. Lucky if they show up at all."

46

Brad's laughter was a little hollow and disoriented, but it passed the man's inspection.

"You know," Brad swung his plan into action, "I did see a couple of young guys running down that alley a few minutes ago. They looked kinda cut up."

The man's eyes widened with excitement. "Are you serious, man?"

"Yeah, I wonder if they stole that van," Brad planted an idea.

"Holy shit, I bet that's them!" The man hurried over towards the others with the latest information.

Brad could hear their "oohs" and "ahhhs" as they circled the man. He glanced around, and when he was satisfied of the group's distraction, he reached into the back of his pants and pulled out the screwdriver. With a few quick twists, Brad had taken the license plate off and stuffed it down his pants. Before the group could turn back around, he had already slunk away down the backstreet.

The pain in his leg had begun to creep its way up Brad's spinal cord as the pill started to wear off. Each step hurt more than the one before it, and his pace slowed. By the time Brad limped up to his front door, the light had begun to wane. His white T-shirt was soaked with sweat, and there were drops of blood on the sleeves from Brad wiping his forehead. He had thrown his hat away shortly after beginning his journey, as it had only added to the heat of an already blistering day.

He stood at the door for several minutes listening to his breath heave in and out. He attempted to quiet himself so that he could hear signs of life from the inside. He prayed that his wife was either gone or asleep: anything to save him from the rampage he knew he was in for. Though he had thought about it during his entire walk, he had been unable to come up with a sufficiently convincing story to cover his wreck.

At first, he decided to tell his wife that his van had been stolen at work. It wouldn't be totally out of the question, except for the fact that it was old and run down and it wouldn't explain his injuries. Also, she could ask for a police report or call his job to confirm the story and he'd be screwed. Next, he thought about saying he was carjacked and that he fought against the assailants, thereby becoming beaten and bloodied. The thought had entertained him and bolstered his spirit for an hour or so. He pictured himself like a Rambo or John Mclean, kicking asses and taking names. He was so fond of the idea, in fact, that he had planned to use it right until he turned onto his street and remembered one thing: he was a total pussy. His wife would never believe he'd do anything more than run or shit his own pants. He briefly considered soiling himself and altering his story. By the time he finally arrived at the door, he was just as confused as he had been the moment after the wreck.

The sun had turned his skin to jerky, and with the loss of sweat and blood threatening his consciousness, Brad decided to accept whatever fate awaited him and opened the door.

He timidly poked his head in before fully entering. The living room was in its usual state of disarray. The floor was littered with dirty clothes, numerous pairs of sneakers, and old newspapers. The coffee table was covered in used drinking glasses, bits of tissue, unread mail, and a tray containing a plastic bag and broken up pot. The musky smell perforating the air suggested the bong next to the tray had been recently used. Brad closed the door and took a step towards the couch, hoping that there was already a hit loaded.

He stopped when his foot bumped something on the floor and he bent to pick it up. Before he even read the label, he knew it was an empty bottle of cheap wine from the nearby liquor store. It was the same bottle he had brought home two nights ago as an apology for......something he couldn't remember doing. He was about to set the bottle down, when glass exploded to the side of his face. Brad fell to the ground, his leg pounding, his hands clutching shards in his cheek, and moaned.

"Where the FUCK have you been!" Her shriek was more of an accusation than a question.

Brad raised his head towards the distorted figure of his wife towering above him. He blinked away tears and rubbed glass out of his face.

"What the hell is wrong with you? You could have killed me!" Brad's voice was a mixture of anger and desperation. He now knew what he was in for.

"Shut the fuck up!" she waved another empty beer bottle menacingly towards her husband. Her erratic stance told Brad that she had emptied the entire bottle of wine that day.

"I've been at work, where the hell do you think?" Brad attempted to pull himself off the floor in an effort to regain equal footing.

"Since last night!!!" Her voice was an angry hiss. Brad noticed the pillow and throw scrunched up on the couch.

"Yes, I fell asleep at work." Brad tried to spin the event as a perfectly normal scenario. Didn't everyone occasionally fall asleep in the dairy cooler?

"Are you fucked up again?" Her words slurred as she finally lowered the bottle. Her eyes squinted towards her husband and she took a step closer.

"No, I'm not fucked up again, honey. I told you I was done." Brad tried to put his hands on her shoulders, but she jerked away. She nearly fell over in the process.

"Bullshit! You're lying!" Her eyes were wild with chemical anger.

"No, honey. Nothing but beer and weed, remember? That's what we agreed on." Brad's voice was perfectly angelic. He was trying his best to hide his injuries and calm the raging beast in front of him.

"I don't believe you."

"I promise, baby. I'd never lie to you." Brad waited for the next strike.

She stood looking at Brad, trying to reason through the fog. Her thoughts would simply not band together enough to connect pieces she subconsciously knew were missing. After a moment, fatigue got the better of her.

"Fuck it. I'm going to bed." She staggered out of the room; Brad's sigh of relief was clearly audible. He sat down on the couch and reached for the bong. Before he could find a lighter, she had come back in.

"Gimme the keys. I gotta get something out of the van."

Maxine barely managed to get her car parked at her apartment complex before the knocking noise ended, and the car appeared to die. Though she hoped that wasn't the case, Maxine decided to get up extra early the next day in case she'd have to take the bus to work. She gathered her lunch bag and various other items, and opened her driver side door. She leaned over to the passenger seat and hit the lock button on that door. She had planned on forking over the hundred dollars to get it fixed, but by the time she had the money, something else had broken. Eventually, so many little things had failed on the car, that the door lock seemed inconsequential.

Having secured her vehicle, Maxine climbed the outdoor steps towards her apartment. Along the way, she could hear a couple screaming and yelling at each other. She heard the sound of a plate breaking and the woman crying, but Maxine ignored it and kept walking. It wouldn't do any good to call the police anyway. They had never shown up before. They never did.

Balancing her wad of bags, Maxine pulled keys out of her purse and unlocked the front door. She entered the dark room and found it odd. She normally kept at least one light on at all times; she felt safer when she could see everything at a glance. Maxine set her belongings down on the floor and fumbled for the light switch. She could barely make its shape out on the moonlit wall. When she finally flipped it up, nothing happened.

For a moment, she wondered what was wrong. She pulled up the calendar in her mind and cross referenced all the dates of her bills and paychecks. After brief analysis, she realized she had sent the electric bill in a week late. She had hoped they wouldn't notice, or at least wouldn't turn the power off. With a sigh, she closed her door and made her way to the kitchen.

She had moved into the apartment nearly fifteen years ago, just after she had left her husband Raymond. As teenagers, they had fallen in love and faced a bright future. Raymond worked in a warehouse; it was blue collar work, but it paid the bills. They shared a small house in a working class neighborhood for seven years. They spent their evenings and weekends with neighbors, playing card games and making dinner. They were well-liked and poised to start a family. Maxine had always looked forward to having children of her own, and recreating the childhood she had experienced.

At some point, and she never could figure out exactly when, Maxine noticed that Raymond was spending more and more of his weekends "at work." He would usually tell her that things were busy that time of year or some other story. At first, she was excited for him. More work meant more money, perhaps more responsibility. She hoped that all his hard work would bring him a promotion.

The kitchen was pitch black, save for a sliver of moon light that cut its way through the blinds on the windows. Maxine's dark glasses obscured most details, but she still found her way to the drawer easily. She had walked this route so many times that she could have done it in her sleep. She dug around the drawer until she found a box of matches and made her way over to a small table. The flame burst lit the kitchen well enough for Maxine to grab the nearest candle and light it. She went around the apartment, lighting each candle she kept for such an occasion.

The air in the apartment was stale and humid. Sweat stuck to her clothes and she felt disgusting. She could still smell Larry all over her. She lit a candle in the bathroom and turned on the bathtub faucet. She clapped her hands when water shot out and began filling the tub. She could hardly wait to wash the scent of Larry's cheap aftershave from her body. She wondered if he really thought it kept people from noticing the whiskey that was usually on his breath.

Raymond's drink of choice had been vodka rather than whiskey. He would stumble in late on weekend nights and immediately collapse into the bed. Maxine was worried that he was being worked too hard, and decided that she would talk to him about it. Each time she brought it up, he laughed and told her it was ok. They could use all the money he'd be bringing home as soon as this job was finished. After the third conversation, Maxine grew suspicious and began to keep closer tabs on her husband.

She suddenly noticed that things began to disappear around the house. At first, it was small things, like watches or rings, that would reappear a week or so later. She initially thought that she was simply misplacing the items, but now she was seeing the truth. The day that she found the television missing, she decided she'd had enough and went to Raymond's job to confront him. She nearly fainted from embarrassment when she was told that her husband hadn't worked there for several months.

The water chilled her skin as Maxine stepped into the bathtub. She leaned back against the tiled wall and let out a sigh of relief. Maxine closed her eyes and listened to the soft soul music coming from the battery powered radio she had brought into the bathroom. Static clung to every note, and the volume was stuck on a level just loud enough to make out the song, but it was good enough for her. She sang along to the words and dripped water onto her face.

She and Raymond had danced to these songs so many times. During their first years together, he had bought a record player and they would sit in the dark and listen to all of their old albums. She felt close to him, then. Maxine wiped a tear from her eye as she recalled the last night they had spent together.

She had sat awake all night; pacing around the living room as her blood boiled. How could he have lost his job and not told her? How could he be out pawning all the things they owned, and never let on that something was wrong? Where was he spending all his time, and when was that going to change? Each question spiraled inside Maxine's mind until it spawned a hundred new questions. By the time she heard the key in the door, she was furious.

"Where the hell have you been?" Maxine jumped up and stormed toward her staggering husband.

"Where do you think? I told you I been at work," the words were held together only by will power; they sounded slurred and rehearsed.

"At what job?" Maxine's voice grew louder. "I know you don't work at the warehouse anymore. I know you haven't worked there in months! When were you going to tell me?"

Raymond stared into Maxine's eyes. She could see the lies forming, but he knew he'd been caught. Her breath heaved loudly as she waited for an answer. Part of her hoped that he'd come up with something good and actually convince her that everything was alright. The rest of her wanted to hit him.

"We'll talk about it in the morning. I'm going to bed." Raymond turned towards the bedroom and began to unbutton his shirt.

"No, we won't! We'll talk about it now!" Maxine followed behind him, refusing to be waved off.

"Baby, I'm tired and I wanna get some sleep," the agitation in Raymond's voice edged his words.

"Not until you tell me what the hell you've been doing with your time and our money!" Maxine grabbed Raymond's shoulder to spin him around. The power of his fist shocked Maxine as her nose busted and she collapsed.

Raymond stood above Maxine as she cowered on the floor. Blood gushed from each nostril; ruining the blouse she had on. Tears filled her eyes as she held the front of her face. Raymond's shocked expression did little to calm her.

"Baby, you know I didn't mean to," Raymond took a step towards Maxine in a futile attempt to apologize.

"Get away from me!" Maxine hissed through a mouth full of blood.

"But, baby, I didn't mean…" Raymond bent down to help Maxine up.

She pushed him with all her might; in his drunken state, he went down easily. Maxine hauled herself up. She was determined to walk despite the pain emanating from her face. She sobbed as she made her way towards the front door.

"Where the hell you think you going?" Raymond had made it to his feet.

"Stay away from me!" Maxine cried in desperation as she continued towards the door.

Raymond's hand spun Maxine around and held her firmly in place. His feral eyes bore through her skull. She had never seen him this way, and she was terrified.

"Listen to me!" Raymond yelled, "I told you that I don't wanna talk about this shit tonight. I just wanna go to bed. All right? But I can't go to sleep unless I know you not gonna do something stupid behind my back. Do you understand me?"

Maxine stared at Raymond as if she'd never met him before. He was a different man from the one she married; even the one he'd been just a few months ago. Though she was scared, she had to know what was going on. She silently prayed for God to help her through the next few minutes.

"Raymond," Maxine's voice shook as she spoke, "I need to know what's going on..."

Before she could finish, she was on the floor again. The side of her face stung, and the room was spinning.

"God dammit, woman!" Raymond's voice was booming, "What the fuck is wrong with you? Why can't you just get your ass into the bed and be quiet til tomorrow?"

Raymond began stomping around the room, rubbing his head with his hands and cursing his wife. Maxine laid perfectly still on the floor, holding back her sobs and trying not to throw up. Raymond yelled and ranted for almost an hour, though little of what he said made sense. Maxine waited until she finally heard him slam the bedroom door before she stood up.

As quietly as she could, she crept out of the house and made her way over to a neighbor's. At their suggestion, she called the police to file a report. She sat on their couch for hours, weeping as she came to terms with what had just happened. Though they were consoling, the neighbors were unable to provide much beyond a place to stay for the night. After a few hours, Maxine gave up hope of even the police coming by to take a report. She realized that she could never return to that house or her old way of life. Her love for Raymond, her dreams of having a family; all of it had been shattered. The next day, when she was sure he was gone, Maxine snuck into the house and grabbed the few items she could carry. She took no photos with her and never spoke to Raymond again. Maxine later learned that he had been stabbed to death during a dice game shortly after their divorce.

Maxine laid in her cold bath, fighting the heat and the painful memories that had crept up on her. She reached over the side of the tub and opened her cigarette case. She pulled out a KOOL and lit it on one of the candles. She watched the smoke rings drift from her mouth, into the dimly lit air. She leaned back and took another puff as the song on the radio changed from the Supremes to Otis Redding.

"I've got dreams, dreams to remember..." Redding's mournful voice sang over the distorted guitar.

Maxine wiped another tear away from her eye and exhaled. She thought about her husband, and the future they could have made together. She thought about the broken car that sat out in the parking lot that would probably cost a fortune to fix. She thought about the small dark apartment that she sat in now, covered in cold water just to escape the heat.

"I've got dreams, dreams to remember..." Maxine took another drag on her cigarette and sang to herself in the dark.

Chapter 14

The bell attached to the diner's door announced Roland's entrance to no one in particular. The few patrons kept their heads on their meals, and took no notice as he found a seat in a corner booth. The scent of frying bacon and perpetually heated coffee accompanied the sound of old country songs emanating from the jukebox against the far wall. Roland glanced around; observing each customer's location, and making sure he wasn't being watched.

When he was satisfied with his anonymity, he reached into his pocket and pulled out a disposable pen. He yanked a few napkins from the dispenser on the table, and began jotting down information. His eyes shot up at the sound of a saucer and mug being rattled onto his table. Without asking, the crusty old waitress poured coffee into Roland's cup and walked off. He grimaced at the stale taste of the lukewarm drink.

He read through his scribble, adding notes here and there. Everything seemed to be in order, and he sighed with satisfaction. His stomach growled, demanding attention, and he looked around to find the waitress. She dumped a plate off at the table across from his and kept walking. He assumed the grunt aimed towards him meant that she'd be back.

"Fucking shit hole," he grabbed the laminated menu from behind the condiment bottles. He wondered exactly how tough the steak would be if he ordered it.Of all the greasy spoons he'd eaten at, only one had been worth a shit.

Years before, Roland had wandered up to a similar diner. His face was cut and bruised; he limped toward a table and plopped down. His muscles ached, and his stomach rumbled. His eyes darted around the room, and his hands shook. He forced himself to look normal; he even smiled when the waitress approached.

She was a young woman, probably in her mid-twenties. She was short and too thin, her face already beginning to show signs of a hard life. Her fake plastic fingernails were chipped, and her white sneakers were stained with grease. Her stare was distant, as if focusing on anything for too long would cause her to break down into tears.

"What can I get for you?" Cassie, as her name tag revealed, kept her eyes on her order pad.

"Coffee." Roland kept his eyes peeled on the door.

"Coming up." Cassie turned towards the counter, but stopped mid-step. "Are you ok?"

"Fine." Roland's finger tapped the menu nervously. He wondered if he should make a break for it now, or wait until Cassie walked off.

"We have a bathroom back there if you need to clean up." Cassie pointed towards a door next to the counter.

Roland nodded his head slightly, hoping it would shoo her away. When she went to fetch his drink, he reached into his pocket and pulled out a couple of single dollars and some loose change. He searched the rest of his clothes, unsuccessfully, for more money. It would appear his first free meal would be a slim one.

"Here you go," Cassie returned with his coffee. "Are you ready to order?"

"Just this," Roland ripped a sugar packet open and poured it into his cup.

"Alright, then," Cassie walked to another table and took an order.

Roland sipped his coffee and thought. He had no money, nowhere to go, and no way to get there. What the hell was he going to do now? He considered his options throughout the night as he watched the other customers come and go. He stared at their leftovers, and contemplated trying to snatch them when Cassie wasn't looking. Eventually, he was left alone with the waitress. Though he could feel her eyes on the back of his head, he kept his gaze aimed at the window.

"Here," Cassie's voice startled him. She slid a plate of eggs and steak towards Roland.

"What is this?"

"I see you looking at the other tables." Cassie sat down across from Roland. "You obviously don't have any money,"

Roland unwrapped the silverware from the napkin holding it, and took a large bite.

"Why do you care?" His voice was thankless.

"It's the Christian thing to do," Cassie's voice was earnest.

Roland snickered and took a sip of his coffee.

"That's what my mom would say, anyway," Cassie blinked.

Roland finished his meal in just a few bites. Perhaps it was the taste of freedom, but he thought the overcooked steak was fantastic. He turned his mug up, and drained the last of his coffee.

"Well, you're mom sounds like a smart lady," his words were laced with ridicule.

"My mom's dead," The blunt force of Cassie's words surprised him.

Roland wiped his mouth and stared at the waitress for a moment.

"I'm sorry. If it makes you feel any better, my parents are dead, too."

Cassie opened her mouth, but shut it quickly. She took a deep breath to steady herself.

"So, what's your story?" She tried to change the subject.

Roland's lips curled into a cruel grin.

"It's a long one. One I'm sure you wouldn't be very interested in hearing," Roland turned his cup around in his hand a few times.

"You look like you been in a fight," Cassie got up to grab a pot of coffee. She returned, and set it in front of Roland.

"My whole life," Roland poured himself another cup.

"I know what you mean," Cassie's voice cracked.

Roland stared at the girl without speaking. He noticed light yellow patches protruding just below her short sleeve. Scars dotted the folds of her arms.

"Something tells me that you do."

Cassie squirmed slightly at the attention.

"It's hard to trust people, isn't it?" Roland lowered his voice. "You stick your neck out there sometimes, only to have it chopped off by someone you thought you knew."

"Is that what happened to you?" Cassie's eyes widened with child-like wonder.

"Yeah, that's what happened to me," Roland stared into his coffee cup thoughtfully. "What about you?"

"Oh," Cassie became shy, "I guess I've been fightin', too."

"Boyfriend?" Roland cocked his eyebrow.

"Husband, boyfriends, dad… you name it." Cassie rubbed her arms. "I'm not very good at picking men."

"I'm sorry," Roland lowered his eyes.

"Don't be. They were assholes," Cassie grinned at the obscenity. "Besides, it looks like I won."

"Well, here's to the assholes we've kicked," Roland raised his coffee mug. The two chuckled.

"You've been so kind to me already tonight," his words were soft and gentle," I wonder if I could ask one more favor."

She suddenly looked uncomfortable.

"You don't have a cigarette, do you?" Roland laughed to put her at ease.

Cassie's face brightened and she reached into her apron. She pulled out a pack of light cigarettes and handed them to Roland.

"Here, you can keep these."

"Thanks," Roland's finger brushed across Cassie's hand causing her to blush slightly. He let his eyes linger on hers.

"You know what we need?" Cassie finally broke the charged silence. "A couple of pieces of apple pie!"

Cassie jumped up from the table and headed toward the counter. She took two pieces from a refrigerator and put them on a plate.

60

"Do you want whipped cream?" she was giddy and awkward.

"Sure," Roland stood up and walked toward the counter.

She grabbed a canister and shook it. A small blob spurted from the nozzle, and then nothing.

"I'm gonna have to grab another…" Cassie stopped abruptly. The knife pressed into her throat, causing a trickle of blood to run down.

Roland held it steady as he ripped her apron off. He grabbed a wad of loose bills from the pocket and stuffed it into his own. His hand patted her body down until he heard the jingle of her keys. He shoved his hand into her pocket and yanked them out.

Tears streamed from Cassie's eyes. Her entire body began to shake uncontrollably.

"Why?" She choked the word out.

"We're not all saints like your mom," Roland butted the handle of the knife into Cassie's temple, knocking her instantly to the floor. He tossed it to the ground and left the diner. With sixty dollars in ones, and a run-down Nissan, Roland headed out into the night.

"There's no smoking in here," the ragged words creaked from the crusty waitress's mouth.

Roland looked up from his half-eaten steak to meet her jagged face. Wordlessly, he dropped the cigarette into the cup of stale coffee. He grabbed his notes and stood up from the booth. The waitress stepped aside as he pushed past her.

"Fuck this rat nest," he kicked the bottom of the door open and stormed out of the diner.

Roland slammed the door of his stolen car and drove off. As he cursed to himself about the waitress, he thought about his notes and his next step. He was sure he had everything, but decided to take one more look around. He drove the few blocks and circled around the MegaSaver parking lot once again.

Chapter 15

Agony tore through Brad's knee and instantly woke him. He jerked himself up and clutched his wounded limb. He heard a clatter from the back room of the house. It was overly loud and obviously designed to irritate him. Brad could hear things being hurled around and imagined the worst.

A notebook lay next to his leg, and Brad could only assume that it had been thrown onto him. He turned it the right way around to read the hurriedly scrawled message. He wasn't sure, but it appeared to read: "FUCK YOU. I'M LEVING." Brad attempted to locate the missing letter when his wife charged into the room.

"What is this?" Brad stared at the suitcase and duffle bag in his wife's hands.

"What the fuck do you think it is?" She stared daggers into his face, awaiting his response.

"You're leaving me?" Brad's voice was confused and apprehensive.

"Yeah, asshole. I am." She set her bags down and walked into the kitchen.

"But.....why?" Brad's leg was stiff and throbbed as he tried to move it.

"You have got to be fucking kidding me!" Her voice raged from the kitchen. The refrigerator door opened and closed.

Brad once again tried to stand, but his leg would not allow him to.

"I am so sick of your shit!" His wife stomped into the living room and cracked open her can of Coors Lite. "You waste our money on pills and pot. You are never home, and when you are, you're barely here. I can't tell if you're awake or not half the fucking time. And don't even get me started on the fucking van! Do you even have any idea where you fucking left it?"

She took a gulp from her canned beer and stared at Brad. His eyes widened for a second, and then everything became clear. The van! Oh, shit. The van!

"Oh shit! The Van!" Brad wasn't sure if the first one had actually been spoken.

"Jesus Christ!" She leaned back and killed her drink. "You don't even fucking remember doing it, do you?"

He nodded his head, though the details were still a little fuzzy.

"I'm going to stay with friends for a while. Don't call me." She returned to the kitchen and threw away her empty can.

"But, honey," Brad attempted to explain his actions. "Don't go! I'll change, I promise. I'll throw everything away and we can start over."

His wife returned to the living room and picked up her bags.

"Too late. I already did that for you."

She walked towards the door and opened it. She turned for a last look; he was already checking the coffee table cabinet for his stash.

"Get sober, asshole and maybe we can talk."

Brad turned to see the door closing behind his wife.

Chapter 16

Leonard Best walked slowly and with a slight limp down the grocery store aisle. He pushed a broom in front of him; gathering bits of paper and opened chip bags that hadn't been paid for. The young workers around him laughed and cursed. They bragged about the cashiers they took turns having sex with, and mocked each other's physical attributes. Above him, a light flickered, threatening to extinguish itself completely. The air conditioning rattled in a unnerving manner. Leonard shook his head and wondered what the world was coming to.

All day long, he had smiled at customers and tried to make polite conversation. He was mostly ignored or bossed around by rude customers. He never let it get to him, though in his heart, he knew this was not the same business he had spent so many years in. Leonard sighed as he picked up a snack cake box with several cakes missing.

As he rounded the corner, he was hit by the smell of vinegar. His face flinched and his nostrils stung. He walked a few feet to the mess he knew he would find. Sure enough, a gallon size jar of pickles lay smashed on the floor of aisle twelve.

His knee popped as he bent down to sweep up the broken glass. The rattle in the ceiling stopped as the AC turned off. Leonard could instantly feel the imposing heat encroaching. A drop of sweat fell into the shards. It reminded him of...he dropped the dustpan as memory overtook him.

It had been a hot summer night, and the air conditioning had gone out at the Third Street market. Gladys Best was feeling faint and sat on a stool behind the register. She dabbed the sweat from her forehead, and drank from a glass of ice water. The small fan beside her did little to ward off the imposing heat.

Leonard wiped his own brow and resumed sweeping the floor. He was damp and sticky, and was looking forward to going home to a cold shower and lemonade. The day had been slow; with most people leaving almost the instant they entered the building. Leaving the front door open had done little for the temperature inside.

"How you feeling Gladys?" Leonard had noticed that his wife was not able to deal with the heat as well as he had during the day. He decided to sweep up this last pile and call it a night.

"I'm making it," Gladys was never one to complain.

"I know better than that. How about we close up shop and go home?" He bent to scoop up a pile of dust.

"That sounds good to me," She stood to make her way to the front door. She swayed slightly and caught herself on the counter.

Leonard stood to help her.

"Are you okay?" He held his wife by the arm.

"I'm fine. Just a little dizzy." She steadied herself and flashed Leonard the smile that he had fallen in love with. After all these years, he still found her every bit as dashing as she had been when they were young.

He heard the bell on the front door jingle; he turned to see it close as a young man entered. Leonard felt a twist in the pit of his stomach.

"Excuse me, son. Our air conditioner's out and we decided to close for the night," Leonard took a step that put him between his wife and the teenager.

The young man was tall and dark skinned. His hand was shaking slightly, and he seemed nervous. He was wearing blue jeans and a shirt with the sleeves cut off. His clothes were dirty; the padding of his shoes was barely hanging on.

He and the teen stared at each other for a second. Leonard took a step forward.

"Son, did you hear me?" his eyes never wavered from the youth.

65

Anger radiated from the young man's body as the barrel of the gun slammed across Leonard's face. He instantly fell to the floor, and Gladys screamed.

"Shut up, bitch!" the young man aimed the Smith and Wesson towards her. Tears ran from her eyes, and she held on to her husband.

"What do you want with us?" Leonard took a deep breath and wiped the blood from his temple.

"Get up and give me all the fucking money in the register!" the barrel of the gun danced as the boy's hand trembled. Leonard worried it might go off by accident.

"Sir, we haven't made anything today. It's too hot," Gladys wept in fear.

"I told you to shut up, bitch!" the boy grabbed Gladys by the hair and threw her to the ground. He aimed the gun towards the back of her head. Leonard's heart skipped a beat.

"I ain't playing with you, old man. Get up and get me the fucking money!" the kid's eyes bore into Leonard's.

Leonard's head nodded, and he raised a hand towards the teenager.

"Alright, alright," he conceded. "It's not much, but you're welcome to it."

Leonard slowly pulled himself up. He could hear Gladys' muffled sobs coming from the ground. The teen's eyes never left him.

With a couple of button clicks, the register drawer opened. Before he could take anything out, the young man had pushed him aside and grabbed the cash out. The boy was furious with the result.

"Eighty seven dollars? Is that all you've got?"

"I'm sorry," Leonard begged, "that's all we made today."

Doubt crossed the young man's eyes as he quickly plotted his next move. Leonard stared at the boy for what seemed an eternity. He pictured himself being killed that night. He imagined the agonizing phone calls his children would receive, and the pain they would feel over his death. He thought about his wife being forced to sell the store and trying to piece her life back together. He saw her standing over his own, bleeding lifeless body, and his eyes filled with tears.

"Please, son. Just take it and go." Leonard choked the words out and prayed.

He lowered the gun and jumped over the counter, towards the door. He knocked a display of jarred pickles over; glass and vinegar spread across the floor.

"I'll take this shit tonight, old man," the teen said as he pushed the door open. "But you're gonna have to do better than this next time!"

The young man was out of the door and racing away before Leonard could round the counter and lift his wife up. Her eyes were full of tears and her mouth bled. Leonard stroked her hair, telling her everything would be alright. Gladys' mouth began to swell, and he could see that she had broken a tooth. Leonard pulled her close to his chest and held her.

A tear fell from Leonard's eye and into the pile of broken glass. He wiped it away and took a deep breath. He hadn't thought about that night in years. It was one memory of his time with Gladys he was happy to forget. He couldn't imagine why he would think of it now.

"Attention shoppers, the time is eight o'clock and the store is now closed," Terrence's voice sounded across the aisles.

Leonard flinched, but shook it off. With a feeling of fear he couldn't explain, he went to the back to grab a mop.

Chapter 17

Terrence breathed a sigh of relief as he locked the entrance door to the store. It had been a crazy day, and he was glad that it was finally over. He'd had a cashier call in, a stocker walk out, the deli worker had sliced her finger open, and he had gotten into an argument with a customer over turkey necks. Add to that a backroom full of stock that he had to help put out, and he was beat.

Larry had been no help at all during the day. He had vanished into his office hours ago and wasn't responding to pages or phone calls. Terrence had worked with Larry long enough to know to leave him alone and let him wallow in whatever he was pissed about. Terrence decided to make his usual walk through the store and get the last minute straightening done.

The front area of the store was a disaster. Carts full of returns were piled at the registers. Pieces of cardboard and other trash littered the floor. Maxine marched up and down the registers, barking at her cashiers to hurry up their money counting.

"Maxie," Terrence's voice was tired and irritated, "You got it up here?"

"Yes, darling, I certainly do," Maxine's voice was sugary sweet and condescending.

"Yeah, I'm sure," Terrence said under his breath as he headed towards the back of the store.

On each aisle, he grabbed things that were out of place and tried to find their spots on the rack. He pulled product forward and made sure the shelves at least looked full. He corrected problems that the teenage employees tried to hide, and berated them silently for doing so. This job wasn't difficult. It rarely required much brainpower, and it paid decently. Terrence took comfort in the daily routines, and was thankful he had them. Other managers had come and gone, seeking flashy careers, but Terrence held steady. He'd had enough excitement for one lifetime.

"Dammit," His foot crunched broken glass. He slid his shoe across the floor to wipe the vinegar off. He sighed heavily and turned towards the back room to grab a mop and broom. As he did, he nearly collided with Leonard Best.

"Oh, excuse me," Leonard laughed and took a step back.

"Oh, no sir," Terrence's voice went up slightly in pitch. "It's my fault. I should look where I'm going."

"I was just going to clean up these pickles," Leonard held up the mop and broom to Terrence.

"Good man. I was just coming to find those!" Terrence was happy that someone actually took a bit of pride in their job.

Leonard swept up the glass as Terrence held the dust pan. Terrence avoided eye contact as he dumped the broken pieces into the waste basket that was already in the aisle. Leonard began mopping the vinegar off of the floor, when he noticed a piece of gum squashed next to it.

"These kids today, I swear," Leonard chuckled. "Bet they'd learn to throw stuff away if they were the ones that had to clean it up."

"No doubt, sir," He watched as Leonard struggled to scrape the gum off the floor. Terrence reached for the mop. "Let me see that just a second."

The handle brutally struck the gum, raising it off of the concrete. Terrence angled the mop in just the right way to completely remove it without leaving a residue.

"Wow, you never been a janitor, have you?" Leonard laughed at Terrence's expertise. He smirked but didn't laugh.

Seven years earlier, Terrence had been mopping floors at the state penitentiary. Every day for months, he would wake up at five am, stand outside his cell for the morning count, head to breakfast with the other inmates, and spend the next six hours mopping the prison floors.

When he had first arrived, he was an angry young man. He was full of self-righteousness and rage. He had never considered himself a criminal. He was soldiering against a broken system that never gave him a chance, and that routinely stomped others like him into the ground. Every dollar that he took, every car that he stole was collateral damage. He was a stranger in a hostile land, just trying to survive.

During his first year, he shot his mouth off to anyone who gave him a glare. Rarely did more than a few weeks go by that he didn't scuffle with someone in the yard. Even the guards were targets of his acid tongue; however he knew better than to put his hands on them. One, at least, had decided to teach him a lesson.

One morning, Terrence stood in the rec area of cell block C. His mop swathed across the floor without haste. It was still early, not even seven am, and Terrence was tired. As usual, he replayed key events in his life; especially the one that had landed him here. If he had just run a little faster, ducked around a different corner....

"Hey faggot!" A voice from behind him broke Terrence's concentration. He turned to face a large Mexican man named Jesus. Terrence felt a moment of panic, but he refused to show it.

"You talking to me?" Terrence moved the mop in front of him.

"Yeah, fucker. I'm talking to you." Jesus was over six feet tall in his white "wife beater" shirt. His broad muscles were covered in tattoos. Names of rumored murder victims ran across the creases of his flesh.

Terrence's eyes held Jesus's. The air between the men grew heavy and volatile. Their muscles tensed, and their stances tightened. They were two vicious dogs in the moment before they lunged for each other's throats.

"What you want with me?" Terrence forced his voice not to crack.

"You been talking shit to everyone around here, and I think someone ought to do something about it." Jesus took a step towards Terrence.

"Oh yeah?" Terrence's grip tightened on the mop handle.

"Yeah," Jesus pulled a knife from his pocket. "And it's gonna be me."

Terrence felt his heart race as he realized that one of the guards must have let this asshole out and given him a knife. He made a list in his mind of all the suspects. It was long and contained just about every guard's name in prison. Perhaps he should have kept his mouth shut more often.

"Listen, man, you need to think about this shit before you do it," Terrence had a moment of doubt in his ability to fend off the man nearly twice his size.

"I thought about it already, holms" Jesus's eyes were sadistic and cruel. "And I decided to cut your fucking tongue out."

Before the sentence could process in Terrence's mind, Jesus was flying towards him with the knife. Blood burst from the Mexican's nose as it collided with the mop handle in Terrence's hand. Jesus hit the floor on his back and clutched his face. His moans were furious and rabid. Terrence cracked the mop handle down on the man's face with rancor. A part of him delighted in the brutality of his actions.

Suddenly, Terrence was flying across the air with a splitting pain in his head. His back smashed the concrete floor with a hard thud; his head hit and momentarily disoriented him. Another blow to the stomach brought him around. A second Mexican with tattoos was standing above him with his foot digging into Terrence's abdomen. He recognized him as a member of Jesus's gang.

Terrence grabbed the man's foot and twisted with all his might. The man lost his balance and wavered slightly; just enough for Terrence to move out from under him. Terrence threw a few unsuccessful punches, and was quickly restrained

71

by the newcomer. With horror, he watched Jesus standing in front of him, spinning the knife in his hand.

There was little pain at first as the blade tore into his side. For an instant, only the rush of blood indicated he had been punctured. A moment later, he was face down on the floor, unable to move and barely aware of what was happening around him. He vaguely heard the sounds of yelling and felt someone rolling him over. He was nearly certain he was looking at the smiling face of a guard as the world went dark around him.

"You okay?" Leonard's voice was heavy with concern.

Terrence looked up from the former mess of pickles. He was sweating and his hand was shaking. He noticed his knuckles were red from the tight grip of the mop handle.

"Oh, yeah," he was breathing heavily. "Yes, sir. Just tired."

Terrence handed the mop back to Leonard. The elder man looked worried, and stood awkwardly without speaking. Something in the man's eyes scared Terrence. Was it recognition? He forced himself to pull it together.

"Let's go ahead and wrap it up for the night, alright? It's been a long day." Terrence and Leonard smiled at each other, though neither was at ease.

Chapter 18

"What the fuck is this shit?!" Larry spat the words as he threw the memo across his desk.

He stood and paced around his office. He stared out of his window and watched his employees scramble around with usual idiocy. He saw his stockers and cashiers push brooms over the same areas, and ignore the misplaced frozen food left thawing on surrounding shelves. Larry rarely stayed this late at work anymore, but his mind was frenzied with anger, and he couldn't bring himself to discuss the situation with his wife.

He turned to his desk again and looked at the memo. A cry of disgust escaped his lips, and he yanked his bottom drawer open. There, atop the manila folders with all of his employees' personal data, lay his private bottle of Jack Daniels and an 8 oz rocks glass.

Larry poured himself a large shot and tossed it back. He slammed the glass down and glanced to make sure it hadn't broken. He noticed a drop of whiskey on his fingertip and licked it off.

He stood once more, bottle in hand, and paced around the office. He stopped at the end of his desk and looked back down at the offensive memo. He poured another healthy shot and downed it.

He snatched the memo up and stared at it again. Just the first line made his blood boil: "From the Home Office." His eyes lifted from the page and he surveyed the room. THIS was the home office, not some fucking cubicle farm five states away. He didn't give a shit who signed the checks or bought the product. THIS was where the big decisions were made, and HE was the one who made them. Larry walked to the far wall of his office and removed a framed photograph. He stared at it as the memo crumbled.

"Can you believe these fuckers?" Larry beseeched the photograph of his grandfather. "Can you believe what they want to do to our store?"

He remembered the day his grandfather had opened this store. It had been thirty years ago, when Larry was twelve years old. His hair had been longer, and the suit he was wearing was too big on him. He remembered complaining about the ceremony; it was too hot and he was missing his favorite show on television: Charlie's Angels. Besides, how exciting was a new grocery store going to be?

Jonas Prescott, Larry's grandfather, had owned several small convenience stores over the years, and had made a lot of money through them. Over time, his ambition outgrew his small stores, and he decided to open Prescott's. From day one, the store was a success. It catered to the neighborhood's wealthy residents; featuring brand name, high quality foods and a fine bakery. Jonas ran the store with a big heart and genuine concern for his fellow man; customers and employees alike. In fact, Jonas' funeral, eleven years after the store's opening, was the largest in the city's history. It was even better attended than the man who had beat Jonas in the city's previous Mayoral race.

Walter Prescott, Jonas' son and Larry's father, carried on the family business, though he mainly rested on his father's laurels. His standards fell short of Jonas', and he was happy to hold the course, rather than improve. Over time, the neighborhood began to change. The affluent customers began moving further east into the growing suburbs. The product line changed; favoring cheaper generic brands, as customers became more likely to brandish food stamps than charge cards.

Larry Prescott inherited the family business when he was thirty-three years old. Neither Larry's academic or professional career had been outstanding up to that point. He had spent almost seven years in college, switching majors nearly every year, before finally dropping out altogether and going to work at an office supply store. Larry's temper and constant need to be right prohibited him from rising above his stock boy position. He frequently argued with managers and asserted his opinions despite their objections. His tenure with the company ended when he threw his name tag at his boss and stormed out in a cloud of obscenities.

Having no other options, Larry went to work at his father's store as an assistant manager. He was not particularly well liked by the employees, and his undeserved title caused a minor uproar. Most of the staff had been hired by Jonas Prescott, and only tolerated his grandson out of respect.

One day, he arrived at work to find a note on his father's desk. It explained that Walter was no longer happy with the job or his marriage and had decided to move away with the floral manager. Larry was not surprised, as he had ignored his father's flirtations with women for years. He was surprised, however, to find that the letter was naming him as the new store manager, effective immediately. His first task was to replace the number of employees who walked out when they heard the news.

After hiring a drove of inexperienced teenagers who would work for minimum wage, Larry set about to rebuild his family's name. Unfortunately, his business skills were not sufficient to keep the store out of bankruptcy, and he was forced to sell to the MegaSaver chain. This decision had caused a schism in his family, and he was nearly disowned. He had almost been laid off during the sale; it was only his ability to bullshit that kept him in power. To this day, however, he resented any influence the corporate office exerted on "his" store.

His eyes perused the lines of the memo with increasing difficulty. He was now up to four shots of whiskey and having trouble reading. However, his anger had not subsided, and he continued cursing the page.

"Due to slowed sales and drops in profit...." His voiced slurred the words for no one in particular to hear. Larry crumpled the memo and threw it into the trash.

Who the hell were they to pass judgment on him? He had given the past eleven or so years of his life to this store. He had spent all that time building a team that respected him, that loved him. He had formed the bonds with his customers that kept them coming back, month after month. It was his blood, sweat, and tears that now held the store's foundation together. Had he not given enough? He envisioned his body crucified above the front door, hanging from the "We Double Coupons!" sign, and a crown of register tape circling his head.

Larry pulled the memo out of the garbage can and threw it to the ground. His glazed eyes locked onto the paper, and he crashed his foot precisely down on the target. He pounced up and down on the page until it was a flat wad. His middle fingers blazed hate towards the memo, and his voice bombarded it with obscenities.

"You motherfuckers! You stupid motherfucking, cocksucking cocks!" Froth dangled from Larry's mouth, and a sliver of spittle drooped down. "You're not coming into my store, and trying to take it away from me, you mother fucks! NO! NO NO NO NO! FUCK YOU!"

Larry stomped one last time on the page and then collapsed into the couch next to him. His limp hand dropped the bottle of Jack to the floor, and his eyes began to tear up. How could they do this to him? He rubbed his eyes and pictured the hell that was brimming on the horizon.

"First, comes this bullshit sale," he said aloud, "and then comes a new manager. I know it! I fucking know it!"

"You know what?" a startled southern voice stuttered at the doorway.

Larry quickly jumped up and turned his head. Maxine stood just inside the office, her eyes wide and bewildered.

"What's going on here, Larry?" concern hung to every drawn out syllable.

"Oh, Maxie, it's awful." He did not even attempt to hide his anguish from her.

"What's wrong, baby?" Maxine took a place next to him on the couch; she cradled his balding head in her lap and hugged him close.

76

"These fuckers from corporate are coming to launch some new sale campaign," sobs nearly muffled his already garbled words. "They're gonna try to take the store away from us, Maxie. You know they've been looking for an excuse to get rid of me for years!"

"I know, baby," she lied, "but you know they ain't never gonna do it. You're the glue that binds this place together. They know that. You ain't going nowhere, honey."

He stared up towards the haze that was Maxine. He reached up and removed her glasses so he could (kind of) see her eyes. For the first time, he saw a kind, motherly composure to her face. He took comfort in her arms and felt safety in her lap. She was exactly what he needed.

His lips were pressed against hers before he realized what he was doing. Once again, she returned his affections, and their bodies turned to embrace each other. Larry's lips trailed their way around Maxine's neck and shoulders; his hands caressed her inner thighs and calves. As he brought his fingers up towards her crotch, he suddenly stopped.

"Where is everyone else? Can they see us?" Larry asked with sudden alarm.

Maxine smiled broadly and lifted her shirt off. "No, baby. I sent them home fifteen minutes ago. It's just you and me."

He stood and began to remove his own clothes. His face was bright with hope; his eyes filled with desire. His hand reached towards his desk and touched a button. The store was instantly filled with the light saxophone sound of Dave Koz playing over the intercom. He unbuttoned his shirt and swayed to the music.

"Do you like it, baby?' Larry tossed his shirt playfully to the ground. His wavering hand reached to undo his belt and zipper.

"Oh yeah, honey…" Maxine smirked as she slid her Capri pants down to the floor.

After fidgeting for a moment with his khakis, he stepped out of them. His hand pressed against the desk to stabilize himself. He stood, clothed only in his white boxers and black socks, staring at Maxine's naked form. The darkness of her skin excited him, and the smell of hand lotion set his olfactory nerves ablaze. He remembered their tryst in the hotel room, and his body responded accordingly. Larry's hands gripped his extended waist band, but held fast for a moment.

"Are you sure you like it, Maxine?" Larry's voice was coy.

"Yes, honey, you know I do." Maxine pinched the nipple at her side and moaned.

She reached up and pulled Larry on top of her. Her chocolate hands slid his white boxers away from his pale white buttocks. He reached down to feel her dampness.

Larry pressed his mouth to Maxine's ear and whispered. The tip of his penis was resting just outside the lips of her vagina. "Tell me, Maxine. Tell me you like it."

Suddenly, he thrust inside her sending a shudder through her body.

"Oh, yes Larry! Yes Larry! I like it! I like it!" Maxine's whole body convulsed with ecstasy. "Oh my God! This jazz is so smooth!"

Chapter 19

A subtle queasiness sat in Brad's stomach as he approached the old midtown house. He wasn't sure if it was nervousness, withdrawal, or the gas station burrito he had eaten on the walk over. In any case, it wasn't helping his situation.

Brad limped his way up to the chain link fence that surrounded the house. He paused for a second, took a deep breath, and walked through the gate. He kept his eyes towards the ground, and avoided contact with the group of people smoking outside the doorway. He felt both self-conscious and arrogant; he wasn't some junkie from off the streets. Somehow, he felt as if he were better than everyone here. Brad went through the front door and into the meeting room.

For a moment, he stood at the entrance, trying to get his bearings. The room was large, and filled with rows of old wooden chairs. Many were in bad shape, and he wondered if they would break if he tried to sit in them. He located one in the back corner and sat down. The smell of day old coffee and stale cigarettes filled the room. There were inspirational posters hanging on the walls, and a list of twelve steps towards sobriety. There was a quiet chattering of people as they greeted each other, offered advice, and gossiped about the well-being of missing members.

"Fuck this," Brad said to himself. The whole situation was unnerving, and he wanted no part of it. He didn't need a program to help him quit anything. He was fully capable of doing it alone, and that's what he was going to do. He stood to leave when he felt a hand slap his back.

"Brad!? What the hell are you doing here?" Brad turned to greet the smiling face of Alex Sanders.

"Alex?" Brad was confused and embarrassed to be noticed.

"Yeah, man, it's me! How the hell are you?" Alex's hand rested on Brad's shoulder, trapping him in his place.

"Uh, well…." he was forced to sit as Alex took a seat beside him.

"Oh, shit. Not too good, huh? Yeah, I guess you wouldn't be here otherwise," Alex looked around the room to see who else had arrived.

"Yeah, I guess. You, uh, come to meetings?" he had no idea what to say.

"Occasionally, you know," Alex's eyes shuffled around as his knee bounced. "Court thing, man."

Brad nodded his head and felt his stomach turn. This had all been a mistake. He shouldn't have even come here tonight. Maybe, he could make up an excuse and leave. He could say he was going to the bathroom and then just head out. In the corner of his eye, he watched Alex's knee moving and grew irritated. He opened his mouth to make his escape, when a woman took the podium.

"Alright, ladies and gentlemen. Let's go ahead and get started." She greeted the group with a warm smile. Brad exhaled loudly.

For an hour, he listened to people share their stories. There were lawyers who lost their families and homes, people who had lived in the streets, and the occasional housewife who had overdosed on Xanex or Oxycotin. Most speakers had regularly attended meetings, though there were a few that hadn't. When asked if anyone new wanted to share, Brad lowered his eyes to avoid being spotted. Alex's knee never stopped moving, and he never paid attention. Finally, the same woman from earlier brought the meeting to a close.

Brad was relieved as people stood up to leave. Some part of him felt ashamed and embarrassed to be in the same room with these people; though not for the reasons that brought him there. Complete waste of time, he decided.

"Hey man, I'm going to smoke." Alex slapped his shoulder. "Come on."

The night air was humid and hot; clinging to Brad's clothing as he limped through the doorway.

"So, you get anything from any of this shit?" Alex blew smoke into the air.

"Not really," he shook his head and watched the people around them. He spotted a woman across the yard crying and noticed that another group of women hugged and comforted her. He also noticed that there were a few people dressed in suits and ties, and a few others that seemed to have their lives on track.

"Yeah, me either, man." Alex laughed and took another drag. "I tried to get my company to send me to this fucking rehab villa, but...no dice. I guess after your third time, it's whatever's free. You know what I mean?"

"I'm just trying this out to make the wife happy." Brad continued watching.

"Ah, there it is! I wonder if anyone would come to these things if other people didn't make them." Alex smirked.

Brad looked at Alex. It had been fifteen years since they had last seen each other. He remembered all the times that they had skipped class together and hung out smoking dope or tagging teacher's cars. During his junior year, Alex had been his partner in crime. Brad never had a senior year, a fact that hadn't really bothered him until this moment.

"Yeah, well I should get going." Brad suddenly felt sad.

"Me too. Where you parked?" Alex looked around the parking lot.

"My car's in the shop," Brad lied. "I had to walk up here."

Alex chucked his cigarette to the ground and reached into his pocket. "Hang on a second, brother. I've gotta get this paper signed and I'll give you a ride."

He pulled a pamphlet from his pocket and laughed.

"Here," Alex handed Brad the flyer, "Maybe you've got better insurance than me!" Brad glanced at the picture of the resort and absently stuck it in his pocket.

Brad thought about leaving, but the pain in his knee argued against it. Sweat was already dripping from his face, and he decided sitting in an air conditioned vehicle was worth listening to Alex.

"Ready, buddy?" Alex returned with another lit cigarette.

"Let's go." Brad walked towards Alex's car with him.

"Great. I gotta make a stop before getting you home. Hope that's alright."

"That's alright." he got into the passenger side of Alex's car, and watched the crying woman wipe her face and thank her friends.

Chapter 20

Leonard Best opened the door to his small apartment and stepped inside. After locking the door, he made his way to the kitchen and took a can of Coca-Cola out of the refrigerator. Returning to the living room, he plopped down into his favorite recliner and cracked open the drink.

Leonard took a heavy swig and leaned back in his chair. His legs rose into the air and his back settled into the cushion. It had been many years since he had spent this much time on his feet. He winced as he kicked off each shoe; the muscles in his back knotted, and his legs began to tighten.

He briefly contemplated turning on the television, but decided that he was too tired to pay attention. Besides, he had no idea what was on this time at night; it had been years since he stayed up this late. He sighed as he realized that he would have to adjust his schedule; five am to nine pm wouldn't work with his new job.

As he took another sip, Leonard thought about how difficult his first day had been. Not so much the physical aspects; he could still push a broom with the best of them. It was the memories that had made it so hard. Every time he said hello to a customer, or put an item on the shelf, he expected to see Gladys by his side. Each time he turned to face someone else, his heart broke slightly.

This was the first time since he was a young man that he was working without his wife, and it affected him in ways he had not been prepared for. He missed the small space that they had shared together, and the life it had brought them. The items were the same, though there were more of them, yet the entire feel of the business was different. Leonard hoped that he could cope long enough to pay off his debts.

Leonard finished his drink and pulled his feet back to the ground. His body ached, and exhaustion was fighting to overcome him. As he moved to throw his empty can away, he stared at the apartment surrounding him. It hadn't changed in years, but something seemed different today. It felt empty, lonely.

As Leonard made his way to the bedroom, he stopped at the fireplace mantel. He delicately picked up a framed picture of his wife and stared. It had been taken the day they got married; she was dressed in her long flowing gown. Her smile was broader and brighter than it ever had been before. Leonard's eyes moistened with tears, and he kissed the top of the frame; his hands quivered as he replaced the picture.

He climbed into bed as his body thanked him. The soft mattress wrapped itself around his sore limbs. He could feel sleep falling quickly upon him. He barely even noticed the loud music booming from the cars below him, or the young men shouting obscenities from the street. Leonard rolled onto his side and rubbed the empty spot next to him. As usual, he said goodnight to the woman he loved, closed his eyes, and saw her in his dreams.

Chapter 21

Maxine clutched the back of Larry's desk as a moan erupted from her lips. Her eyes were closed tightly, and sweat covered her face. Behind her, Larry pounded away with an unusual amount of force. His hand gripped her unleashed breast as the other swayed back and forth with each thrust. Her legs were beginning to tremble, and she leaned forward for balance. She felt the first twinge of soreness beginning to form between her legs. She could also feel Larry's testicles slapping her thigh. Finally, she felt his body tense up and then the warm rush pass from him into her.

Larry fell into the couch and pulled his boxers up. His face was soaked, and his heart was beating rapidly. He breathed in and out quickly as he embraced the calm exhaustion that had overtaken him. He laid back and closed his eyes, forgetting the troubles of his day. A few latent drops seeped out and caused a wet spot to form in his underwear.

Maxine's legs tensed and her arms were slightly bruised. The skin on her forearms burned from sliding across the top of the wooden desk. For a moment, she rested and stared out of the window towards the empty store. She pictured the pitch black apartment that she would be heading home to shortly. She could already feel the warm air wrapping itself around her throat and cutting off her ability to breathe. She coughed in anticipation and pulled up her Capri pants.

"God damn, Maxie. You've got one hell of a twat on you!" Larry's voiced beamed as his head rested against the couch. He smiled broadly and took a deep breath.

Maxine fixed her bra and shirt; she pulled a pack of cigarettes from her pocket. She angrily noted that she only had two left and couldn't afford more until she got paid later that week. She flicked the lighter forcefully and lit up. Larry raised his head and stared at Maxine with mild surprise.

"You want me to put it out?" The tone of her voice had already made it clear that she wouldn't.

"I just didn't know you smoked," Larry snorted and leaned forward. He put his hand out.

Maxine exhaled smoke and took out the last cigarette. As she placed it in Larry's hand, she made a show of crumpling the empty packet and throwing it in the trash.

"That's my last one til Friday," Maxine took another drag.

Larry inhaled. He coughed as the menthol burned his throat.

"Here," Larry pulled his wallet from his back pocket and opened it. He handed Maxine a twenty dollar bill. "Now I won't feel bad if I don't finish this.'

"Sorry, I didn't have any Marlboros or Camels, or whatever it is that white people smoke," Maxine chuckled as she took the money and put it in her pocket.

Larry stamped the KOOL into the bottom of his shoe and threw it into the trash can. He straightened his shirt as he stared at Maxine.

"What do you have against white people, Maxie? I mean, aside from me?"

Maxine took a deep drag and exhaled it purposefully.

"It ain't that I got something against white people; I just don't trust them is all." Maxine looked around for something to put her cigarette out in.

"Maxie, I'm gonna give you some advice," Larry's voice became fatherly and condescending, "Black, white, brown, yellow-it don't matter what the color of the skin is. For the most part, people are just stupid creatures looking for somebody to show them what to do."

"Really?" Maxine's countered with skepticism.

"Really." Larry grabbed the butt from her, stomped on it, and placed it in the trash. "Most people are just ignorant sons of bitch's who are constantly trying to find someone to lead them."

"And what about the ones who aren't?"

"Well," Larry smiled, "We're the ones telling everybody what to do."

"I see," Maxine studied Larry's face. She wondered if he was just spouting off at the mouth, or if he really believed all the bullshit he was spewing. "Where do I fit in?"

Maxine thought about all the times she had flaunted her disrespect for him. She pictured herself ignoring phone calls and pages.

"Maxine, my dear, you are definitely one of the leaders."

"Yeah, well, it doesn't feel like it most of the time," Maxine's voice deflated his rhetoric.

"What do you mean?"

"I'm just saying that it's hard to feel like a leader when you're sitting in a dark apartment, waiting for your next paycheck to turn the lights on." Maxine wiped a bitter tear from her eye and turned towards the window. She cursed her own display of vulnerability.

From behind her, Maxine heard a click and turned around. She watched as Larry opened the store's safe and took out a small lock box. He took a key from his pocket and opened it. She stared in amazement as he took the plastic deposit bag from the lock box and removed three hundred dollar bills from it. He stood and handed them to Maxine.

"Will this help?" Larry's voice was soft but decided.

Maxine, unable to speak, took the money and nodded her head. She stared at the bills as if they were the map to a vast treasure. She blinked quickly, wondering if they were a figment of her imagination.

"Are...are you sure?" Maxine cleared her voice and met Larry's eyes with her own.

"Yeah, take it." Larry quickly resumed his brisk tone.

Maxine stuffed the money into her pocket before Larry changed his mind. She couldn't wait to take it to the power company in the morning. Just the thought of being able to see inside her apartment brought a smile to her face.

"Thank you, Larry." Maxine said with genuine gratitude.

"No problem. I'll walk you out." Larry opened the door to his office and stuffed another illicit hundred in his pocket. Maxine was sure it would be converted to whiskey at the nearest bar.

Maxine walked out, dreaming of a new life full of running cars and electricity. She pictured herself in a small house in a decent neighborhood. She even envisioned herself climbing the corporate ladder from supervisor to assistant, and maybe, even store manager. She saw a better day coming down the road, and began to plan on how to get there.

Chapter 22

The headlights of Terrence's car pierced the darkness and illuminated the county road. His radio was barely audible above the noise of the tires running across the pavement. Terrence stared straight ahead while the air conditioner poured cold air across his face.

Why was he here again? What was he looking for? What the hell did he expect to find out here in the middle of the night when he should be at home with his wife? Was he gloating? Was he making sure this road knew that he had beaten it? Was this his big "Fuck you!" to life? Or was it something else entirely? Was he looking for the unquiet souls haunting the highway? God knows there should be a few wandering this stretch of land.

Terrence asked himself each question over and over again as he drove. He often found himself on this dark road. He would usually make up some excuse about working late or running to the store when his wife groggily questioned him. At first, she seemed unnerved by it, but these days she had grown used to it. She would sleep, and he would drive. In the morning, he would be lying next to her, and that was good enough. He was happy with her, and it appeared that she understood that.

After the attack, Terrence had awoken in the prison's hospital wing. He was bruised and beaten, and his abdomen was held together by thirty six stitches. At some point, during the three weeks he spent in the bed recovering, Terrence learned that he had been "saved" by a guard who was wandering into a deserted area for a smoke break. The guard just happened to notice two inmates who had somehow gotten out of their cells and were beating another to a pulp. His timing had been perfect; a few seconds more and Terrence would have been killed. The knife had torn through his side and nicked a couple of organs.

As Terrence recuperated, he began to question everything. He replayed the same events in his mind that he always had; this time, however, they were different. He used to see only greed and entitlement in the faces of his victims. He used to believe that they had each been born with more than their fair share. He thought he deserved a piece of their fortune to set the playing field even. Now, every time he remembered the faces of people he'd robbed, he saw the horror. For the first time in his life, Terrence felt genuine fear.

While he recovered, Terrence believed he was safe. As soon as he was returned to his cell, though, he knew he'd be an easy target. The next time he mopped the floor in some empty part of the prison, he wouldn't be lucky enough to end up in the hospital; he'd leave prison in a body bag. Therefore, he decided that his only hope would be to apply for work detail where he would be surrounded by guards and other inmates in an open space. The day he was transferred back to his cell, Terrence made the request.

The following morning, he awoke at 5 am as usual. Instead of grabbing his mop, however, he was placed in a van with five other prisoners. Shackled together at the leg, they swayed back and forth as the van made its way past the prison walls and out to the county road.

"Your first day?" One of the inmates broke the apprehensive silence.

"Yeah," Terrence eyed the man suspiciously and kept his guard up.

"You're the kid that got beat up a few weeks ago, right?"

"What's it to you?" Terrence glanced around for something to defend himself with.

"Hey, man, I'm just making conversation." The inmate laughed and raised his hands to show he wasn't holding anything. "Don't worry. I'm not trying to fuck with you."

Terrence nodded slightly. He didn't trust anyone, especially a white guy who liked making conversation. He decided to keep an eye on him.

The van eventually stopped, and the back doors opened. The inmates were lead out to a long stretch of isolated highway. Each side was covered in tall, overgrown grass; which, in itself, was covered with garbage and litter. Each prisoner was handed a large garbage bag and a poker. They were arranged side by side, and began to walk through the grass grabbing garbage and placing it in their bags.

"So, you healed now?" The white man was paired with Terrence.

"Yeah, still a little sore, but okay." Terrence answered, keeping him in his peripheral vision.

"Yeah. I got stabbed once," the man jabbed an empty two liter bottle and shoved it in his bag. "In a bar fight in Reno, you know before…"

"Where'd he get you?" Terrence pulled a cigarette packet off the stick and tossed it into his bag.

"*She* got me in the leg, right under my left nut." The man laughed curtly and bent over to pick up an empty cereal box.

"She?" Terrence stopped to look at the man. He couldn't help but laugh.

"Yeah, she was an unruly bitch," the man dumped the box and laughed at himself.

"You must have done something to get stabbed in the nuts." Terrence shook his head.

"Just under the nuts, don't exaggerate." The man reached down to pick up a cigarette butt. He placed it in his pocket. "And yes, I did a lot of shit."

Terrence laughed as the man told him a wild story about the stabbing. As the day wore on, and the trash bags were filled, the men shared stories with each other. Some of them were true, many of them apocryphal tales passed down by liars. In any case, they entertained each other until the guards loaded them back into the van. As they approached the prison walls, the laughter subsided, and a knot began to form in Terrence's stomach. He secretly prayed that he'd make it through the night.

The back door to the van opened and the inmates were taken out and unshackled. Each man waited to be lead back to his own cell. As he turned to go, Terrence looked at his new friend.

"Hey, man. Good talking to you today." Terrence's voice betrayed his dread.

"You too, buddy. See you in the morning." The words were a command rather than a statement.

"Terrence," he extended his hand to shake the other man's.

The man raised his arm, revealing the snake tattoo around his wrist. He took Terrence's hand and firmly shook it.

"You can call me Roland," the man said.

Chapter 23

Brad awoke to the buzzing of a fly and a splitting headache. He slowly opened his eyes to ease the pain of morning light burning his retinas. He didn't recognize the ceiling he was staring at. It hurt to move, so he stayed completely still. Where the hell was he? A stirring next to him forced him to turn his head.

He realized he was lying on a mattress in the middle of someone else's living room. There was an unfamiliar woman next to him, barely covered with a sheet. Brad slowly sat up, and looked down at himself. To his surprise, he was completely naked except for the used condom still wrapped around his flaccid penis. He stood, cautiously, all too aware of the searing pain in his knee, and tried not to wake his strange companion.

Brad found a pile of clothes next to the mattress that appeared to be his. He put on his underwear, and limped down a hallway towards a door that he hoped led to the bathroom. He was relieved to find a toilet awaiting him. Brad lifted the seat, and lowered his boxer shorts. He quickly rolled the condom off and threw it into bowl. He gasped as his eyes caught the reflection in the mirror. He flushed the toilet, and hesitantly moved in for a closer look.

Amongst the healing bruises from the car wreck, he saw that his face was a mural of smeared lipstick and smudged makeup. There was also a spot of dried blood caked under his right nostril which he quickly washed away. Without warning, vomit choked its way up Brad's throat; he barely had time to reach the commode.

As he heaved, there was a knock at the door. He instantly stopped. Brad was a deer in headlights, awaiting the hunter's shot. Alex's voice broke the silence.

"Hey man, you alright in there?" his voice was more annoyed than concerned.

"Alex?" Brad was puzzled. What the hell had happened?

"Hey champ, breakfast is on the stove." Alex knocked one last time and walked away from the door.

Brad closed the toilet seat and sat down for a second. He replayed the previous night's events in his mind and desperately tried to put the pieces together. He remembered going to the meeting, he remembered bumping into Alex, he remembered standing outside smoking......and Alex was supposed to give him a ride home. Brad rubbed his face as he finally remembered the "stop" the two had made.

"Come on, man! It'll be fun!" Alex pulled into a parking spot and turned off the car. He was smiling and thumping the steering wheel along with the music.

"Man, I need to get home. I've gotta be up tomorrow for work and everything." Brad protested.

"Don't worry. We'll just have a drink or two....unwind....see some titties, and then go home. I'll have you back before eleven." Alex had already jumped out of the car and closed the door before Brad could respond.

Alex walked boldly towards the door of the Platinum Pony as Brad reluctantly followed. He had never been to a strip club before. It wasn't that he was morally opposed to them; he had just never had the opportunity or inclination. He spent most of his nights curled up with his wife and bong, in front of old TV reruns. Most of his ties with friends had fallen by the wayside some time ago. He hadn't even been inside a bar in nearly three years. He approached this one with caution.

Alex threw the door wide open and held it for Brad. The two men entered and approached the bored-looking girl at the counter. Brad panicked for a moment when she asked for ten dollars apiece for the cover. Alex slapped a twenty on the counter, and the two kept going.

"Wow, man, you didn't have to do that," Brad was nervous and apologetic.

"Nonsense, my friend!" Alex was right at home, "We haven't seen each other in years, and you're in bad shape. You pay for nothing tonight, you hear me?"

Brad attempted to thank Alex, but he had already disappeared behind the entry curtain. Loud music pulsated and shook the walls of the club. Brad pulled back the curtain and timidly stepped in.

He was instantly awestruck by the half-naked women walking past him. Some carried trays filled with drinks, some just walked up to tables and sat in men's laps. Every woman smiled at Brad as she passed him, each taking mental note to find him after he'd ordered his minimum second drink. Alex waved from a table against the wall.

"Over here, man!" Alex yelled over the rap song playing. A slightly overweight dancer pranced naked around the stage. She shook her pointy nipples as men around her threw dollar bills at her feet.

Brad made his way to the table and sat down. His posture was stiff, and he felt out of place. The only woman he had seen naked in the past five years had been his wife- the same wife that was at her friend's house, probably taking a marker to wedding photos and looking for divorce lawyers in the phone book.

"Just two drinks, right? I gotta get home soon," Brad yelled into Alex's ear.

"Yeah, yeah." Alex had already begun to ignore Brad in favor of the busty waitress who now stood at their table.

Within moments, the two men each had a beer and a shot of whiskey in front of them. Alex handed Brad his shot, and they clinked glasses. Brad couldn't make out exactly what the toast was and shouted to Alex to repeat it.

"I said... HERE'S TO FLOATIN ON A SEA OF TITTIES!" Alex yelled. Brad chuckled despite himself and downed his drink.

"That's my boy!" Alex laughed and patted Brad on the back. "Let's have a little bit of fun for a change!" Alex took out a wad of one dollar bills and handed a few to Brad.

"What do I do with these?" Brad was confused.

Alex nodded towards the main stage. The overweight girl had left, and a new song began to play. The stage went dark for a moment, and the lights pulsed to the beat of the music. A tall, thin woman with dark red hair and star tattoos on her wrists paraded down the stage's walkway. Her body moved with sensuality and determination. She wrapped her legs around the pole at the center of the stage and swung herself around. She removed her top and tossed it behind her. Her breasts were full and large; each nipple was pierced. The woman slid herself around on the floor like a snake for a moment, before rolling on to her back, and sliding off her thong. She pulled herself back up on the pole to expose her shaved pubic area to the crowd.

Alex gently pushed Brad towards the stage. He awkwardly approached the beautiful woman as she plucked a bill from one of the regulars. Smelling fresh blood, she made her way over to Brad. He held the dollar towards her as if he was feeding a wild creature. The woman smiled, took the money, and slid it down her leg. She hooked it beneath a strap in the high heel she was wearing. Brad stood, watching her naked body in front of him. The dancer leaned onto her back again. She lifted each leg, giving him an unobstructed view of her vagina. As he handed her the wad of dollar bills, she grabbed the back of his head and pulled him to her. She wrapped her legs around Brad and grinded him for a few seconds.

As her song was coming to a close, she released him and turned back towards the pole. He stumbled to his table. The scent of her perfumed thighs lingered in his thoughts. He found two more shots of whiskey waiting for him and drained them. Alex clapped his hands and laughed. Brad smiled and sat back down in his seat.

They watched the various women as they danced across the stage. Brad had become enchanted by their nudity; time was an element he no longer considered. Beer and whiskey kept coming, and he drank without consequence.

After a few hours, Alex had convinced one of the naked women to sit with him and have a drink. She kept telling him that she could lose her job, but made no effort to hide her actions. Alex eventually began kissing the woman, and completely ignored Brad. Just as he was beginning to feel left out, he felt a tap at his shoulder. He turned to face the overweight dancer he had first seen when they came in.

"Yeah?" Brad looked at her. Her breasts were small and pointed in opposite directions. She was short and stocky, but not exactly fat. Her shape was an odd one, and Brad decided that she was probably the lowest paid woman at the club. She stared at him with an expression that was an equal mix of hope and desperation. There was even a hint of resentment.

"Do you wanna tip me?" The girl's tone had already made it clear she didn't expect yes for an answer.

Unable to control himself, Brad burst out laughing. The girl laughed, too, though she wasn't exactly sure why. He turned to Alex to let him in on the joke, but his friend was busy putting his hands under the table, between the dancer's legs. Brad looked back towards the other girl. She had already started to walk away when he gently touched her arm. She looked at him for a moment, and he beckoned her to their table. Within minutes, Brad had his mouth on hers, and Alex was getting the car.

Brad sat on the toilet in his underwear, finally realizing where he was and how he had gotten there. He looked at himself in the mirror and disliked what he saw. He wasn't looking at the man that had gotten married. He wasn't even looking at the man who had left the meeting last night. He was looking at someone who had hit bottom and needed to pull himself up.

He saw the roads that lay before him. He could continue down the one he was on, like Alex, and end up ruining his marriage and possibly dying in a drunk-driving accident. Or, he could fix himself and reclaim his marriage. He decided that it was time to take action. All he needed was a way home.

Chapter 24

The temperature was already 95 degrees, and the sun had only been up for an hour or so. Larry had been to sleep, woken up, and driven to work in less time. His eyes were red and bloodshot as he pulled into the parking lot of the MegaSaver grocery store. He parked his car in his usual spot, and noticed that he was the last to arrive. He recognized the cars of the employees who actually owned them, and assumed the rest had found rides or taken the bus. He noticed a Mercedes Benz parked at the front, and muttered an obscenity to himself.

He opened a bottle of Advil and washed four tablets down with a scalding cup of gas station coffee. He yelped as the liquid ripped a layer of flesh from his tongue; his head began pounding to the rapid beat of his heart. He closed his eyes and forced himself not to throw up. After a moment, he left his car, and quietly shut the door behind him. Quickly, he made his way through the sticky heat, towards the oasis of cold air conditioning inside the store. When he entered, and felt no such relief, he nearly flew into a rage.

"Goddamit, the fucking compressor must have locked up again," Larry loudly announced, paying no attention to the store full of employees milling about. He stomped towards the thermostat and attempted to make out the tiny numbers. He was astounded by what he saw.

"Seventy-five? Who the fuck turned this to seventy-five?" Larry mentally accused everyone he could think of. He forcefully mashed buttons until the thermostat displayed the usual setting of sixty-four.

"Excuse me," an unfamiliar voice caught Larry from behind. "I turned the setting up. It'll help your store save two hundred dollars a week in utilities.'

Larry spun around to find the smiling, good-natured face of Michael Standland staring back at him. He eyed the suspiciously happy man with distrust. A sudden wave of nausea, however, prevented the harangue he had planned to unleash. Michael extended his hand towards his. Larry noticed tiny black prickles of stubble forming on Michael's arm.

"Michael Standland, District Manager of Marketing." His voice was calm, friendly, and yet firm. It was warm and inviting; offering a soothing introduction, yet clearly enforced his authority over the situation. Larry grabbed Michael's hand harder than he would normally and shook it briefly.

"Larry Prescott, Store Manager and former owner." The words sounded hollow and desperate. The title that Larry clung to so tightly was just a notch above ceremonial, and he was constantly afraid of losing it. He realized too late that stating he had once owned the store before bankrupting it only weakened his position.

"Hello, glad you made it," Michael's stare was constant and unflinching. He refused to break eye contact, attempting to form a subconscious link of communication between the two men.

"Yes, well....." Larry was unnerved by the stare and looked away. He saw Maxine standing several feet away, pretending not to watch the conversation.

"Hey, listen," Michael interrupted, "I was going to go over some things before everyone else got here, but I guess we need to go ahead and get started."

Larry was furious at the subtle accusations that Standland was directing at him. Who the hell was this asshole to tell him when he should be at work? He had only found out about the meeting when Terrence called him thirty minutes earlier.

"What do you mean there's a fucking meeting?" Larry's arid voice squawked, "Who the fuck called a meeting?"

Terrence explained that there had been a memo attached to the employees' last pay check with the date and time for the meeting. Having direct deposit, Larry never actually looked at his checks. Had he known, he may have gotten more sleep or drank less the night before. Now, he was talking to some asshole from corporate while his intestines played hopscotch on his stomach. Larry contemplated punching Standland in the face.

Michael slapped Larry's back in a friendly, jovial fashion. It signaled the end of the conversation and directed Larry to his seat with his employees. Michael was already stepping up to his podium before Larry had time to say anything.

"Hey, darling, how are you?" Maxine whispered to Larry as he plopped himself into his seat.

"Fuck this asshole." Larry responded to his Front End Supervisor.

"Alright, thank you guys for coming today," Standland smiled towards the employees. "My name is Michael Standland, and I am the District Manager of Marketing for the Food Lot Corporation."

Larry snorted in disgust at the name; Michael ignored him.

"The reason I'm here today is to tell you about a fantastic new promotion. It's a little program that I came up with, and it is designed to help struggling stores like this one." There were startled gasps from several employees.

Michael stepped from behind his podium and assumed a relaxed position to put everyone at ease. A blank, widescreen television standing behind him reflected the worried faces of the employees.

"Listen guys, I don't want to scare anyone, but the truth is that this store has not been making sales goals for the last year," Michael's eyes glanced towards Larry before moving to the rest of the group. "We all know how rough the economy is right now, and Food Lot has to take a hard look at its family and make some tough decisions."

"Is that true?" Maxine whispered to Larry. She decided the flood of obscenities that were quietly flowing from his lips was not directed towards her.

"Now, I firmly believe that we can turn this store around," Michael comforted the crowd with his voice. "I've seen stores worse than this one surpass sales goals after just one weekend of this promotion."

"I know you're all asking yourselves what this promotion is, and how it's going to affect you," Michael's voice was amused and practiced. "Well, the name of the promotion is *Spend and Win.*"

The reaction from the crowd was less than enthusiastic.

"Here is a breakdown of how everything will work, and how it will help your sales soar!" Michael walked to his podium and clicked a button. The television behind him displayed a sales graph.

For thirty minutes, Michael Standland enlightened the employees with his visions of sales, gross profit, future plans, goals, and revenue. Each topic was accompanied by a graph that was nearly incomprehensible to most of the people looking at it. Midway through his presentation, Michael was interrupted by the sound of snoring. A flash of anger passed across his face as he turned to see Larry asleep and slumping in his chair. Maxine kicked Larry's leg, and he abruptly sat up and coughed.

"I know this is complicated stuff, but try to stay with me guys," Michael admonished as much as apologized for his presentation.

"Excuse me," Larry's voice boomed. His patience for this hairless asshole, and his charts, had reached its end.

"Yes, Larry?" Michael's voice held a hint of fluster. Larry seized on it like a pit bull.

"All of these charts and plans and everything are really wonderful," sarcasm ripped Standland's presentation to shreds, "but what's the point? If you're gonna have a sale, you gotta have a gimmick." Larry smiled as he heard mutters of agreement from the employees behind him.

"Ah yes, the *gimmick* as you call it," Michael clicked a button on his podium, and the screen went past several more charts, "I was actually going to end with that. I suppose now's as good a time as any." There were more mutters of agreement from the crowd.

101

"Alright, amidst all the price reductions and sales that we will implement, we will also kick off a contest at the beginning of the coming week," Michael resumed his smile. "Each customer that spends at least fifty dollars in your store will be entered to win $10,000 in cash."

Suddenly, the crowd was quiet.

"Are we going to actually be keeping $10,000 on the premises?" Larry worried. The other employees paid close attention.

"Only for one night," Michael replied. "I'll get with you on those details, later on. In private."

Larry nodded his head. Damn right he will. In fact, Larry decided to question him as soon as the meeting was over.

"As I was saying," Michael continued, "we will award the prize at the store in front of the local media. It's phase one of a three part advertising campaign that I'll brief you on now."

Standland smiled and clicked to the next chart. He ignored Larry's belch as he jumped out of his seat to run to the bathroom.

"What the fuck?" Terrence stared at the money in his hands. He had recounted it three times, but it was still coming up four hundred dollars short. He took a deep breath and set the bills down. He had them neatly stacked in denominations, beginning with the hundred dollar bills and ending with the ones. He had the coins separated as well; the quarters down to the pennies. He had set the three foreign coins to the side.

Terrence shuffled through the closing paperwork, trying to make sense of the numbers before him. He had done deposits for years without any sort of mistake. He knew that it couldn't be himself. Could it? He was tired from another restless night of driving, as well as the early morning meeting. He picked up his coffee cup and took a huge gulp. He began counting again.

Terrence had conquered his fear of money several years ago. He used to feel nervous handling it; like a recovering alcoholic in a bar. For the first year or so, it taunted him. Each bill rolled around his hands, daring him to "drop" one or pocket a stack. Each urge had been resisted, and after a time, they had finally vanished. He realized, however, that his hands had begun quivering as he flipped through each stack. Once again, the deposit came up short.

Terrence rubbed his eyes and thought. What were the possibilities? A cashier could have counted wrong the night before. No, each person had been signed off on. Perhaps he had missed an envelope or something. No, he had verified each one. Terrence began feeling a pinch in his lungs as he hurriedly flipped through pages again. Finally, he found a clue. He stared at the initials on the last sheet for a moment, without allowing himself to jump to conclusions. There had to be a logical explanation; a clearly legitimate reason for Larry to have shorted the deposit.

Terrence jumped at the knock on the office door.

"Hey, how's it going?" Michael Standland stood in the doorway with a counterfeit smile. Terrence returned it.

"Great, just finishing up the deposit." Terrence forced his voice to remain calm.

"Great, that's something I wanted to talk to you about," Standland entered the office without invitation.

Terrence's heart skipped a beat, and the pain in his chest grew worse.

"As you know, we're gonna be bringing in a lot of money with this promotion," Standland's eyes locked with Terrence's in an effort to convey understanding. "This goes for your daily deposits, as well as the actual prize money."

"Yes, sir. I paid close attention to that at the meeting." Terrence hoped to quell suspicion before it grew out of hand.

"I appreciate that," Standland nodded. "What I'm concerned with is the security of your money here."

"How do you mean?" Terrence hoped that the crack in his voice wasn't noticeable.

"Well, I've talked to Larry, but I wanted to get your opinion as well," Standland's voice became grave with concern. "I need to know I can trust the money here. Have you ever had issues here before?"

"No. Not at all." The words belted from Terrence's mouth.

"Well, take a second to think about this," Standland continued solemnly. "Have there ever been any robberies, cash snatching, drawer shortages? Any issues with deposits or anything like that at all?"

Terrence wondered if he was being set up. He studied Standland's eyes for a moment, trying to locate any landmines he may be about to step into. His teeth grinded and he took a leap of faith.

"Not since I've been here. No." Terrence decidedly shook his head

Michael Standland studied Terrence. A split second before it became uncomfortable, Standland stood and slapped Terrence on the back. He smiled broadly.

"Great! That's what I like to hear." Standland appeared satisfied.

"Anything else I can do you for?" Terrence's voice was a mix of relief and disbelief.

"Not right now, but thanks!" Standland turned towards the door to leave. "Oh, just one more thing. I'll be sticking around until the promotion is over. I rarely get a chance to see these things all the way through, and I think it would be fun."

Standland smiled like a child making his wish list for Santa Clause. Terrence felt obligated to nod, even though he hated the idea.

"It'll be good to have you around," Terrence lied.

Standland rapped the door twice and headed out towards the store. Terrence collected his thoughts for a moment. He didn't like the idea of corporate snooping around. Something was obviously going on, and it would be difficult to keep it under wraps. If Standland caught wind of the discrepancy with the deposit, he would start an investigation. Eventually, the investigation would lead to the police. Terrence shuddered at the idea.

He collected the money for the deposit and placed it back in the blue zippered bag it came from. He filled out his bank slip, with the full amount, and placed it in the bag. Terrence folded the bag neatly and put it in his pocket. He decided to make a quick stop by an ATM on his way to make the deposit. He began trying to figure out a way to explain the withdrawal to his wife and cursed Larry for stealing the money in the first place.

Chapter 26

The coffee was lukewarm and tasted like it was two days old as it rushed down Larry's throat. He set the empty cup down with a hard thump and resumed devouring his eggs and bacon. The last few bites of his waffle sat soaking in syrup. He stared at his plate and resumed his conversation.

"I mean, this asshole thinks that giving away $10,000 is going to bring in money? I mean, where's the $10,000 coming from in the first place?" Larry looked up for a waitress to refill his cup.

"I'm sure they've got all that figured out, sugar," Maxine took a slow sip of her coffee and watched Larry shove another forkful of food into his mouth.

"Please. This stupid son of a bitch couldn't figure out how to change his own underwear without a memo from home office. I guarantee it." Larry became impatient and snapped his fingers loudly. Maxine tensed at the sound.

"Baby," Maxine's voice could have soaked Larry's waffle, "why don't you slow down and chew? You know you gonna choke to death."

"I mean," he ignored her suggestion, "this guy really thinks that keeping that much cash in the store overnight is a good idea? We'll be lucky if the place isn't stormed by fucking armed robbers before we can lock the fucking door to the safe."

"Speaking of money, you don't think anyone's gonna notice our little....arrangement, do you?" Maxine's eyes held on her coffee cup.

The food in Larry's mouth stopped moving. He raised his eyes to meet Maxine's and took a deep gulp. Just then, the waitress appeared with a fresh pot of day-old coffee. Her face was lined with wrinkles, and her uniform stained with jelly. Silently, she poured liquid into each of their cups and walked off. Larry shifted in his seat, uncomfortably considering various options.

"It's fine," he finally spoke.

"You sure?" Maxine stared at Larry with slight disbelief.

Larry swallowed hard and raised the cup to his mouth.

"Yeah, it's fine. I'll make sure." His tone was not reassuring.

Maxine blew steam from her cup and curtly rolled her eyes. She couldn't keep the glint of a smile from passing across her face.

Larry dropped his fork onto his plate and chugged the last of his bitter coffee. He silently burped into his hand. His hangover had finally receded, and he was beginning to feel normal. He looked around the dingy diner for the waitress; he hoped she didn't expect a tip after the service they'd received.

"I can't believe this. Where is that old bitch?" Larry grunted into the air.

"Why are you always so angry?" Maxine scolded him.

"I don't understand how you're not." Larry snapped back. "All the fucking idiots walking around us every day. All the bullshit we put up with. And then pile your money problems on top of that. You should be postal by now."

"Baby, not everyone wears their heart on their sleeve like you do." Maxine wiped her face with a napkin.

Larry turned to deride the waitress again, when he noticed the look on Maxine's face. She looked hurt and embarrassed. He felt that he should say something to her, though he wasn't really sure what. He wasn't used to caring what other people thought or felt.

"I'm uh…." He stammered. "I'm sorry. I didn't mean…"

Maxine's hand reached across the table and touched Larry's.

"It's okay, darling. I know," she sighed.

"I really didn't mean to upset you," Larry continued awkwardly. He didn't know if he should keep talking or not.

Maxine smiled and stroked his hand gently.

"You don't have to keep apologizing, I'm okay."

Larry nodded with satisfaction. He felt like he'd dodged a bullet.

"However," Maxine's mouthed curved into a sly smile. "I know how you can make it up to me."

Larry returned her smiled and pulled out his wallet. He dropped a couple of twenty dollar bills onto the table and led Maxine out towards his car. He pressed her body against the door and kissed her passionately. She moaned slightly, and he opened the door to let her in. Larry jumped into the car and started it in one fluid motion. They kissed once more before pulling out of the lot and heading towards the King Hotel.

Four crisp, one hundred dollar bills slid out of the dispenser of the ATM and into Terrence's hand. The computer voice thanked him a little too loudly for comfort as he shoved the money in his pocket. His eyes studied the area for hidden predators looking for their next fix. He walked quickly and confidently towards his car, just a few feet away, keeping his senses on high alert. Out of the corner of his eye, he noticed a disheveled man stumbling down the street. To his side, he saw a car drive up and park several spaces away. His hand reached for the door and, instantly, pulled it open. He planted himself in his seat and hit the automatic lock button.

The sense of irony was not lost on him. Today, he was a respectable business man, making a deposit for his job. Just a few short years ago, he was on the other end. He could still see the woman's terrified face when he closed his eyes. It was nearly midnight as a young Terrence sat in the alleyway. A long stream of smoke lazily rose from the end of his cigarette. His eyes were centered on the ATM nearby; his hand slid up and down the switchblade knife in his pocket. He shivered slightly and ignored the hunger pain in his stomach. He was tired of waiting and was getting agitated. For the past hour, he had seen nothing but bums and addicts walking up and down the street. He briefly thought about jumping one of them for pocket change, when he saw headlights pull up to the machine. He dropped his cigarette and ducked into the shadows. His heart thumped quickly.

A middle-aged woman stopped next to the ATM and glanced around the empty parking lot. She moved briskly, trying to insert her card while keeping an eye out around her. The machine buzzed at her, and she dropped her gaze to punch a button. Terrence took the moment to pounce.

With shaking hands, the woman turned her card around the correct way and typed her personal ID number. Her eyes rose quickly and darted around. Terrence ducked behind her car; the machine buzzed loudly as it spit money into her hands.

"Hand it over, bitch." The shocked woman turned to face an open switchblade knife. She froze in panic.

"I said, hand it over!" Terrence's voice grew louder as he stepped closer towards her. She slowly handed her purse to Terrence.

"Take it. Please, just don't hurt me." Tears streamed down her face.

"Shut the fuck up!" Terrence snatched the woman's purse and rummaged through it. The money she had just withdrawn wasn't there. "Where's the fucking money?" He screeched.

Terrence looked up and thrust the knife towards her. She screamed in fear and shoved her hand into her coat pocket.

"Here!" The woman yelled and jabbed her hand in his face. His eyes instantly burned, and fire raced down his throat.

"What the fuck!?!" Terrence was blinded, and he thrashed his knife frantically. A sharp pain raced across his forehead as the woman's ring tore into his skin. Terrence collapsed to the ground and cowered.

He rolled around, trying to wipe the mace from his eyes. His tears had no effect, and he was unable to run anywhere to get water. He yelled in agony as he heard sirens close in. He forced himself up, and took an aimless step, unsure of where he was headed.

"Get on the ground, asshole!" Terrence's face hit the pavement hard, and his arms were yanked behind him. The cuffs bore into his wrists painfully, and he was flipped over to choke on his own blood.

An older Terrence put his car into reverse and backed out of his parking space. He hated thinking of that night. He hated it more than the memories of being stabbed, or even his escape. That night, he had been a wild animal. He had told himself then that he was doing it for food. He was doing it to get even with society. In his heart, however, he knew that he had just wanted to hurt people.

During his short, but brutal, life on the streets, Terrence had developed a blood lust that he rarely admitted to. It wasn't enough to take money from people. He had to feel their fear and see their pain. It was a side of himself that he was terrified of. He hoped that the last few years had been kind enough to bury those urges. Every sleepless night told him he could never be sure.

He pulled out of the parking lot and onto the street. He immediately got caught in the unusually heavy morning traffic. He sighed as he looked at the broken, corroded neighborhood around him. There were crumbling apartments that housed poor, hungry people. There were overcrowded schools that offered children little hope of escape. There were abandoned buildings that had become havens for drug dealers and prostitutes. There was a dingy diner with people making out in the parking lot.

The car horn blaring behind him startled Terrence; he realized the light had turned green. He pushed the gas pedal and drove forward. Unable to believe what he had just seen, he quickly turned left into a gas station lot and parked. After a moment, Larry's car passed by the station. Terrence watched as Maxine sucked on Larry's neck from the passenger seat.

"What the fuck is going on here?" Terrence slammed the car into drive and followed them to the King Motel.

Chapter 28

The automatic doors slid open, and Brad sheepishly poked his head in. He looked around to see if anyone was watching for him. He, quickly, stepped in and made his way through the store, towards the stockroom. With his head down and his fingers shaking with anxiety, he keyed his employee number into the time clock. According to the display, he was exactly one day and three hours late.

Brad's head was throbbing, and his stomach was unsettled. He had been sober for a few hours, and it was not agreeing with his body. The cab ride home and the walk to work had been unpleasant at best. Each turn and every ray of sun had done its best to make him vomit.

He took a deep breath. He knew he should make the rounds, fill up his aisles and make sure everything was up to standards. Instead, he went to a phone mounted on the wall. Nervously, he dialed the numbers and waited. Each ring made his head quiver and his stomach cramp.

"Hello?" Her voice was a strange relief to Brad.

"Hey," was all Brad could force himself to say.

"What the fuck do you want? You sober yet?" Her words slid together a little more than they naturally should.

"I'm trying, baby. I really am." Brad hoped the desperation in his voice could convince her.

"I'm not in the mood for *try* dipshit," Brad could hear the distinct sound of a can popping open on the other end. "I need stability. I need consistency! Your shit's all fucked up!"

Brad nodded his head as if she could actually see it. He hoped she had no idea how bad it really was. He could still taste the cheap lipstick from the woman he had awoken next to. He reached into his pocket and pulled out a piece of folded paper.

"Listen, I've got an idea," enthusiasm poked through. "I found a place that I can go to get all my shit fixed."

"A mental institution?" she laughed and slurped her beer down.

"No, it's not like that," Brad paused. "Well, it's kind of like that. It's a place where you go and get help. You stay there for a month, and when you come out, you're well!"

Her laughter cut him to the bone.

"Listen, I thought it was something that maybe we could do together." He tried again.

"What the fuck? Why the hell would I need to go there?" Her voice became a sword, slashing at his heart.

"No, I mean, you could be there for support. That's all I meant." Brad covered his tracks quickly.

"Listen, I need my space for a while. Why don't you call me when you get back from Rehab Mountain, or wherever the fuck you're going?" The conversation ended with a click of the phone.

Brad sighed with a heavy heart, though he was determined not to give in. He stared at the brochure Alex had given him and imagined himself there. The photos looked lavish and relaxing. It seemed like a villa atop a calming forest. It would be like a vacation from their addictions. Brad pictured spending long days lying out in the sun with his wife at his side. They would drink coffee by the lake in their bathrobes. They would reform the bond of their marriage; reestablish a link that they had lost long ago. They would draw a path towards a happy future together. Brad picked the phone up again and dialed the number listed on the paper.

"Cooling Meadows, this is Denise." The lady's voice was soothing and enchanting.

"Uh, yes, uh, Denise." Brad felt like a babbling idiot. "This is Brad. I, uh, I have…uh…problems."

"Yes, sir. I am very sorry to hear that." Denise sounded calming and genuinely concerned.

"Well, it's okay. Because, I want to get them fixed," Brad was trying hard to impress this lady he'd never met. "Me and my wife."

"Good for you. Cooling Meadows is the perfect place to sort out any issues that may be hindering your marriage." Denise was happy again.

"Great, great!" Brad was reassured. "I've looked over the brochure, and I am very impressed by your place."

"Yes, it has everything you could ever want: classes, private counseling, spas, saunas, a pool, and of course, a tennis court. Physical exercise is key in recovery." Denise began her presentation.

"Oh, that sounds wonderful." Brad's head was filled with visions. "The only thing that I didn't see on here is the price."

"Yes sir, we feel it's best to discuss that with our guests." Denise's voice was steadfast and inviting. "You mentioned your wife, sir. I do have a couple's package starting at five thousand dollars."

"FIVE THOUSAND?" Brad was thrown from his imaginary horse. "That covers both of us?"

"No, sir. I'm afraid that would be five thousand each." Denise was unfazed by Brad's reaction.

"Oh, I see." Brad's eyes teared as he let the price sink in. "Thank you very much."

Denise was asking follow up questions as Brad hung the receiver back on the base. His head throbbing, his stomach aching, his dreams smashed; Brad slumped down against the wall. He would never be cured; he would never put his marriage back together. He would die alone and addicted. He reached into his other pocket and pulled out more pills. Without even trying to figure out where they came from, he threw one back in his mouth and swallowed. He may as well dive head first into his fate.

"Hello there." A voice startled Brad, and he stood up.

"Uh, hello." Blinking back tears, he stared into the confident face of Michael Standland.

"My name is Michael Standland. I'm District Manager of Marketing." He extended his hand. "I didn't see you at the meeting this morning, did I?"

"No, I uh, I've been sick the past couple of days." Brad shook Standland's hand weakly. "I'm Brad."

"I'm sorry to hear that," Standland placed his hand on Brad's shoulder. "Well, if you've got a minute, I'd like to run through a promotion that we've got coming up."

"Yeah, sure." Brad could barely focus on Standland's words. A mixture of dejection and intoxication kept their meaning at bay.

"Great. The short version is that we're doing a contest for our customers." Standland began grandstanding.

"Uh huh." Brad was noncommittal.

"Two weeks from now, we will be giving away $10, 000." Standland cast his hook.

The words cut through the fog of Brad's worries.

"Did you say $10,000?" his voice was clear and hopeful.

"Yes, Brad. I did." Standland smiled broadly.

As the two men walked, Standland prattled on about gross profit and revenue. Brad had long ago tuned out. In his mind, he was sipping coffee by the pool and reconnecting with his wife.

Chapter 29

Maxine walked through the door first and made her way to the time clock. Her steps were deliberately nonchalant, her demeanor forcefully normal. She waved at other coworkers, said hello to customers, and pretended that she didn't feel a slight dribble down her thigh. She clocked in and took her place at the registers.

A few minutes later, Larry stomped in. He kept his trademark scowl and said nothing to anyone as he made his way up the stairs to his office. Part of it was for show, part of it was because of the twenty dollars he had just given to Maxine for gas. He hadn't minded helping her out one time, but he began to suspect that a pattern was forming. A twenty here, a fifty there; slowly she would bleed his bank account dry. He had already come up with some creative accounting to explain the hotel bills to his wife. Eventually, she would figure things out and could drag him through an expensive divorce.

With money on his mind, Larry entered his office and walked to the safe. He was trying to figure out exactly what to do about the missing deposit money. Normally, he wouldn't care so much. He could easily shuffle money around to cover it for a few days until the matter was forgotten. Unfortunately, Standland was poking his nose into Larry's store. He knew he had to do something quickly. He opened the safe door, and his breath caught.

Where the hell was the little blue bag? Shit. Shit! Someone else must have taken the deposit to the bank. Fuck. Larry slammed the safe door. The only two people that could touch the deposit besides him were Terrence and…Standland. Terrence could be handled fairly easily. Larry could just yell, or gripe, or somehow turn it into Terrence's fault until he was happy to have it dropped. Standland, however, was another problem. Larry cursed again as he pictured Standland smooth-talking the bank teller about the missing four hundred dollars.

116

He would come back to the store, make a few phone calls, and the next thing you know, the store would be crawling with cops and management. Larry cursed again.

"Everything alright?" Terrence's voice startled him.

"Yes, of course." Larry stared at Terrence and felt relieved to see the blue bag in his hand. He didn't even notice the strange way Terrence was looking at him.

The two men stared at each other awkwardly. Larry couldn't figure out how to broach the deposit subject without giving himself away.

"Did you take the deposit?" Larry finally asked.

"Yep." Terrence continued staring.

"Was...everything alright?" Larry's voice quivered slightly.

"Yep." Terrence stared.

Larry prepared his rant, but was stopped dead in his tracks.

"The deposit all good?" Larry was puzzled.

"Yes, sir. Why wouldn't it be?" Terrence turned the screws.

"I...uh....I was just making sure. I mean, with all the promotions and things going on, I just wanted to make sure." Larry tried to sound as straightforward as possible.

"Everything is good." Terrence finally broke his stare and laid the deposit bag on top of the safe. "Deposit slip's inside the bag."

Terrence turned and walked out of the office. Larry sat for a second collecting his thoughts. He reached out for the bag and glanced over his shoulder towards the window. He pulled the deposit slip out, and stared at the total. It was all there. All of it. Even the four hundred dollars he stole.

"What the fuck is going on here?" Larry set the deposit slip on his desk and pulled a bottle of whiskey from the bottom drawer.

Chapter 30

The air was still hot and sticky, despite the sun having set hours ago. Flies buzzed around, and cars drove by slowly. Roland wiped sweat from his forehead and watched the front door of the MegaSaver. The employees filed out one by one and dashed to their cars. Roland chuckled to himself as he watched the women clutching their purses and darting their heads around. Fuck their purses; he had bigger fish to fry.

He sat across the street from the grocery store in a 2003 Ford Focus as he had done for the past few nights. He counted the number of employees that closed and made note of when the bald man and the black woman left, sometimes an hour or so later than everyone else. He'd rather only deal with one of them, but he could handle them both. The woman might scream a little, but could easily be subdued. The man was short and stocky; the frequent wobble in his step meant his reflexes wouldn't be sharp enough to put up much of a fight.

As the last cautious woman dove into her car and locked the door, Roland hummed to himself and wiped off the .44 in his lap. He liked it to shine when he put it in people's faces. It took the focus off him and usually made them piss their pants. The door to the MegaSaver closed and he slid the cotton ski mask over his head.

He would wait for the employees to drive off and hide beside the door. When the bald guy came out, Roland would put the gun in his face and force him back into the store. If the woman was with him, he would probably have to cold-cock the man first to handle them both. Once they were inside, he'd make the man unset the alarm and open the safe. He wasn't sure if he would let them live or not. Those were the kind of decisions he liked to make on the fly.

Before he could open his car door, Roland noticed the store's inside lights turn off. He stopped and watched. He hadn't expected them to leave this early. He cursed as he saw the door open; he had missed his opportunity. He ripped the mask off his face and flung it into the passenger seat.

Who the hell was that? It wasn't even the bald guy closing that night. It was a taller, muscular, black man. He was glad he didn't try it tonight. This new guy easily had three inches on Roland; there was strength in his movements, and power in his steps. This was a man who would fight back...and win.

The lack of light across the street made it difficult for Roland to get a good look at the man's face, but he looked, somehow, familiar. Roland lit a cigarette and studied him. He doubted it was someone he had robbed; a guy that size would usually have to be put down as soon as Roland encountered him. It wasn't someone he had met on the run. He usually kept to himself and trusted no one.

The man turned from the front door and stepped into the bright light coming from the pole high above the lot. Roland flashed to a night years ago. Broken headlights... twisted metal...flashing yellow... Suddenly, Roland knew the man. He was older, bigger, and more powerful than when Roland had last seen him, but it was him. It was the prison kid.

He watched as Terrence looked around the lot before walking to his car. Terrence moved quickly and took long steps. He was in his car and backing out in what seemed like one motion.

"Fuck the store tonight," Roland thought. There were bigger fish to fry indeed. He started his car, and slid into traffic, behind Terrence.

Chapter 31

The moon was full and low as it lit up the bus stop. The heat in the air was unrelenting; anyone who happened to step outside was instantly drenched in sweat and general humidity. Leonard Best wiped his brow as he took a breath and stepped down from the bus. His left knee was stiff and he could feel his feet swelling. Standing on them for nine hours that day was rougher than he remembered. He would have to soak in a warm bath when got home to ease the pain. Perhaps he could find Epson salt, as well.

He waved goodnight to the driver as he made the four-block walk to his apartment. The heat pressed down on him; his chest began to tighten, and his breath became more forced.

As he limped toward his home, Leonard watched the streets surrounding him. It was a bittersweet experience. He thought of all the friends that had come and gone, all of the birthdays and holidays that had passed. He still remembered the way the neighborhood seemed to shine on sunny days when the buildings were new. He thought of all the time he'd spent raising his children in this community, and how it had been good to him over the years.

He crossed the desolate street; most people had locked their doors as soon as the sun had gone down. During the day, he walked freely anywhere he pleased. This night, however, the neighborhood took a dark and ominous tone. Buildings stood in blackness; broken streetlights having been long neglected by the city. Alleyways and doorsteps were shrouded in shadows; at some points, vague sounds of conversations, and wicked laughter escaped their dark edges.

Leonard stopped at a bench along the sidewalk and leaned over to catch his breath. He removed a handkerchief from his pocket and dabbed his forehead with it. He imagined the cool air of his living room and the cold drink that awaited him in his refrigerator; he decided to trudge on.

As he crossed the second street from his apartment building, he passed the old park. The swing sets were rusted and covered in graffiti. The corroded, busted slides and clubhouses had sharp pieces of twisted metal that kept parents from allowing their children to play on them. So many years ago, Leonard and Gladys had brought their own children here. They had grilled out with other families, listened to music on the radio, and danced into the night. Now, it was more common to find people sleeping on the benches than children playing catch by the sandbox.

As Leonard passed, he noticed a group of teenagers several feet away. Though he could barely hear their conversation, he was shocked by the language they used. He kept his gaze straightforward and concentrated on making his way home. He felt it best to ignore them, and perhaps, he thought, they would do the same.

"Hey, old man!" One of the young men yelled to Leonard. "Don't you know it ain't safe to be walking around out here at night?"

Leonard turned and waved to the boys. He hoped a smile would keep them at bay.

"Hey, old man!" The teenager persisted. Soon, the group had approached Leonard and blocked his path.

"Good evening, fellows." Leonard smiled despite his fear, and the pain forming in his chest.

"Where the fuck you going out here this late, old man?" A different teenager stared Leonard down. The musty sweetness of marijuana smoke rose from the fibers of his shirt. His breath was foul with the remnants of cheap beer.

"Oh, I was just getting off of work and heading home." Leonard's chest began to throb as much as his knee. He could barely force the hot air in and out of his lungs.

"Yeah?" The first hoodlum continued. "Well, I think you better find a different way home. I told you it ain't safe out here."

Leonard's mind raced as fast as his current condition would allow. He was frightened in a way that he hadn't been

121

before in years. Not since that night he and Gladys had been robbed.

Before he could form another thought, Leonard was face down on the concrete sidewalk. The young men laughed with nervousness and sadistic amusement. A cut on the side of Leonard's face began bleeding, and his chest suddenly stopped moving. The young men began yelling obscenities towards him, trying to force him to his feet. Leonard lay on his side, staring at the ground, wondering if this was his last moment.

As he watched the group's shoes shuffle away, he felt one of the boys dig into his back pocket. Leonard's wallet was thrown into his bloodied face after the teenager realized it contained no money.

Alone, bleeding, and unable to breathe, he lay on the sidewalk waiting for help. He closed his eyes, hoping for a siren or flashing lights to come to his rescue. He felt a trickle of air slip into his lungs and attempted to coax more. After several minutes, he regained his breath and accepted the fact that help was not coming.

Chapter 32

Roland pulled up a few houses down from where Terrence had parked. He felt the first twinge of nicotine itch, but decided against lighting up while he could be seen. He flicked his lighter open and closed, impatiently. He had a gnawing feeling of disgust that he couldn't quite explain.

Perhaps it was the suburb he was parked in. It was a calm and serene neighborhood; all the houses were new and built to the same blueprint. Roland could picture the young newlyweds who plopped down their life savings for a cookie cutter house and a chance to start a family. They probably had people over to watch sports, told bedtime stories to their kids, and made love in their newly-furnished bedrooms. All the while having no idea who lived next door to them.

How the hell had the kid made it to this? He remembered the frightened young twenty-year-old who barely talked and kept to himself. Over the course of a few weeks, Roland had gotten the kid to relax and let loose. The long hours spent beside highways and overpasses, sweating their balls off, and scooping up trash were made a little more bearable by the jokes and stories they shared.

The last time Roland had seen Terrence, however, all of that had changed. It was a hot summer day, similar to this one. Roland and Terrence were walking along a county highway, scooping up pieces of an undistinguishable animal and empty coffee cups. Nicotine withdrawal was eating away at Roland worse than usual; he had been unable to score cigarettes in days from his usual source.

"Hey, kid." Roland stabbed another plastic cup marked with an unreadable name. "You got a cigarette?"

Terrence was bent over the animal, holding his nose with one hand and delicately trying to bag its pieces with the other. The stench was foul beyond belief; he held his breath and tried desperately to keep his breakfast down. He looked up at Roland with a green face and glazed eyes.

"Man, you know I don't smoke." Terrence finally dropped the last piece into his clear garbage bag and tied it into a knot. Roland knew he was lying.

"Goddamn, that's some nasty shit." Roland fanned his nose with his hand. "I don't know how you didn't yak over that."

Terrence swayed slightly as his stomach rumbled. Roland caught Terrence's unease and smiled to himself.

"Yeah, man. Something like that would have made my fucking stomach turn flips." He watched as Terrence clutched his gut. "Did I ever tell you about the time I found a cockroach in my salad in the cafeteria?"

"Shut the fuck up man!" Terrence bent over and spit on the ground.

"No shit, man," He ignored Terrence's plea. "I took a bite and noticed something tasted funny. Looked down and saw the back half of that little fucker wiggling in a piece of lettuce right there on my fork."

"Fuck….you….." Terrence had barely spoken the words when he unleashed his morning's meal onto the ground with ferocity. Roland laughed and clapped his hands at the kid's misfortune.

"Man, what the fuck would you do that for?" Terrence looked up at him with anger in one eye and dark amusement in the other.

"Oh, come on, kid. I was just fucking around." Roland laughed. "Besides, you'll feel better in a minute."

"Fuck you. I ought to kick your ass for that shit." Terrence shook his head but couldn't keep the grin away.

"CLAYBROOK!" The guard's voice was stern and commanding. Terrence looked up to see the guard wave him over.

"Uh oh. What the hell's this shit?" Roland kept his eyes on the guard's hands.

"Guess I'll find out." Terrence looked nervous as he approached the guard.

Roland aimlessly poked the ground around him, staying busy as he kept his eyes on Terrence. He noticed the kid's body tense up and his face go pale. He staked his stick into the ground and waited for Terrence to walk back over to him.

"What's going on, kid?" Roland noticed tears in his eyes as Terrence kept his face pointed at the grass.

"Nothing." Terrence kept walking. He stabbed a fast food box with viciousness.

"Bullshit, what's going on?" Roland grabbed Terrence's shoulder and turned the kid to face him.

"That fucking Mexican that kicked my ass is getting out of solitary today." Though he tried to sound tough, Terrence's voice was that of a frightened child's.

Roland looked at the kid and genuinely felt sorry for him. They both understood it would just be a matter of time before the Mexican found a way out of his cell and finished the job on Terrence. Unable to offer any sort of conciliation, Roland patted Terrence's shoulder and silently kept pace with him.

For the rest of the day, they worked without a word. Roland knew that no joke would be funny; no story would entertain them. He thought of various ways to help the kid, but realized they wouldn't work. They were from different cell blocks; they didn't even meet at the same lunch times. The kid would be all on his own against the Mexican and his gang of thugs. In the back of his mind, Roland knew this could be the last day he'd ever see the kid.

As the sun began to set, the prisoners were lead back to the van that would return them to prison. One by one, the men took their seats on the metal benches inside. They were hot and tired; hungry and parched. Most of the men told obscene jokes or ragged on each other. A few planned for the day they would be released. Roland and Terrence sat quietly and listened.

The van moved steadily down the bumpy country road. Though they couldn't see outside, the prisoners knew there were no street lights this far out. Only the headlights from the van itself illuminated the pavement in front of them. Occasionally, another car would pass by, though the road was mainly deserted.

Inside the van, Roland watched as Terrence stared at his own feet. His hands were clutching at his forehead, and his leg bounced up and down. Though he tried to hide them, Roland could hear the quiet whimpers as Terrence fought back tears.

"Listen, kid…" Roland leaned forward so that only Terrence could hear him. Terrence raised his head and met Roland's eyes.

The sound of a car horn suddenly ripped through the air. Before Roland could speak, he was thrown across the van and jerked back by his shackles. There was a deafening noise all around him, as the van tore itself apart. He could hear screams and panic for a brief moment, and then, everything went black.

"Roland! Roland!" Was that his name he was hearing?

Roland opened his eyes to see Terrence leaning over him. He took a deep breath and felt a stabbing pain. He turned his head to cough and a tooth flew from his mouth. There was a heavy weight pressing on his legs, and he could barely move. Although he was lying on his back, he was fairly sure he was staring at one of the van's walls.

"Are you okay?" Terrence's face was covered in blood as a gash in his forehead gushed. He wiped the wound with his hand and pressed hard.

"What the fuck happened?" Roland looked around the twisted metal. He looked down and realized the weight at his legs were the bodies of his fellow inmates. "Can you pull me up?"

Terrence grabbed Roland's arms and pulled with all his might. Eventually, Roland twisted free and stood up. His ankles bled and were bruised; his shackles had come loose from the vehicle. Roland felt his body for further injuries and discovered lacerations all across his chest and stomach. He could feel pulled muscles in his back, but was relieved to find that no bones had been broken.

Terrence had removed his undershirt and was pressing it against his forehead to stop the bleeding. Roland noticed cuts and bruises across his chest, but otherwise, he seemed alright.

The two men crawled across mangled bodies to the outside and were shocked at the scene before them. The van lay on its side; its walls crumbled and the entire front caved in. The battered corpse of a utility truck lay upside down a few feet nearby. Roland imagined the two vehicles colliding on the dark highway; the prison van sliding across the concrete as the utility truck flipped.

He watched as Terrence walked to the truck to check for survivors. He was not surprised when the kid shook his head at the sight. Roland limped to the front of the prison van to look for the guards. Pinned between the driver's seat and the engine block, the crushed remains of the first guard reminded Roland of a splattered watermelon. He winced at the sight, and walked to the passenger side.

Through the shards of windshield, he could see the twisted form of the second guard. Bone poked out through the skin as his limbs contorted into odd shapes. Somewhere, beneath the sound of spinning tires and falling shrapnel, he believed he heard a quiet gasp. Blood covered the back of the guard's head, and Roland bent down to look at the man's face. He fell backwards as the guard's eyes moved up, silently pleading for help.

Roland stared at the blood trickling from the guard's open mouth. As he stood, the guard's eyes moved to watch him. He turned towards the utility truck and saw Terrence trying to take a dead man's pulse. His mind raced as he gathered his thoughts. They were miles out in the country, far from everywhere. It would take at least an hour before someone from the prison realized they were late. Then, it would probably take another hour for someone to reach the accident scene. That gave them enough time to get away.

Roland looked around the wreckage and grabbed a trash pole. He held it to the guard's neck.

"What the fuck are you doing, man?" Terrence's voice was panicked and high-pitched.

Roland stared into the guard's eyes. They were wide with terror and begged him not to do it. Roland's own eyes were cold and vicious.

"You don't have to watch if you don't want."

"You can't kill this guy! We gotta get him some help!" Terrence grabbed Roland's shoulder.

Roland spun around and knocked Terrence to the ground.

"Listen, kid. This fucking pig is the only thing standing between us and freedom, do you understand?" Roland raged. "We do this now, we can run off to Never Never Land and start a brand new life."

"But you can't just kill him..." Terrence could barely force the words out.

Roland lunged forward and stopped when his face was less than an inch apart from the kid's.

"Do you know what happens if I don't? I go back to jail for another seventeen years and rot in a goddamn cell." He spat the words into Terrence's face. "And as for you..... you already know what's gonna happen."

Roland stopped to let the implications of his words set in. Terrence glanced towards the guard and then back up to Roland.

"You go back to that cell, and you'll have a fucking knife through your throat by morning. You hear that, kid?"

Terrence stared into Roland's face. Without realizing it, he nodded his head. Roland returned to the guard and looked into his eyes. The guard's breath was quick; his fingers moved slightly as he desperately tried to force himself away from the wreckage.

"I'm sorry, compadre." Roland licked his salty lips and held the metal to the guard's throat. "But, my buddy and I aren't going back to that fucking jail. Nothing personal."

Terrence flinched as Roland drove the metal deep into the guard's flesh. His breath stopped suddenly and then slowly expelled. Roland grabbed Terrence's arms and pulled him to his feet.

"First thing we gotta do is get out of these orange jumpsuits." Roland nodded towards the utility truck.

The men quickly pulled the workers' bodies from the cab and stripped them. The uniforms were torn and fit neither of the inmates well, but they would sufficiently camouflage them in the dark fields. Using tools from the truck, they removed the remains of their shackles and ran towards the distant lights of the city.

Much later, an older Roland sat in his dark car and looked at the kid, now fully grown with short hair, fake glasses, and a scar across his forehead. He watched resentfully, as "the kid" kissed his beautiful wife at the door to his suburban home in his upper middle class neighborhood. As the door closed, Roland started the car and lit a cigarette. He thought of all the shitty motels he'd been forced to live in over the years. He thought of all the cheap whores and coked-out strippers that had shared his bed. He thought of all the cars he'd stolen and then abandoned. As Roland drove away into the night, he felt a bitterness consume him. He turned onto the highway and, although it was not on the way to the motel, he decided to make another pass by the MegaSaver.

Chapter 33

Terrence pulled into his parking space at the
MegaSaver nearly thirty minutes early. It had been another
sleepless night, and he could find no reason to stay in bed any
longer. He had even stopped for breakfast at the local diner, but
finished his meal quickly and decided his time would be better
spent digging around work for answers to the serious questions
he had.

He entered the store to find all was running smoothly.
Maxine kept the flow of customers moving seamlessly through
the checkout stands. The cart well was fully stocked with
baskets, and the baggers seemed to be on task. He sighed in
appreciation to whatever deity had blessed him with a smooth
morning and headed up to say good morning to Larry.

Terrence entered the office and was shocked to find
Michael Standland at Larry's desk, milling over the deposit.

"Good morning, Terrence!" Standland's voice was
cheerful, yet in control.

"Uh, good morning." Terrence wondered if Larry still
worked there.

"I'm just trying to remember how to do this deposit."
Standland smiled in feigned embarrassment.

"Oh, I can do it if you want." He took a quick step
towards the desk to lend a hand.

"Oh, no. It's alright," Standland smiled as though he
was amused. "I can do it. It just takes me a few minutes to get
back into the swing of things."

"It's okay, I mean, it's my job." Terrence offered once
more. Standland shrugged him off a second time. After a
moment of awkward silence, He spoke up. "So, where is Larry
this morning?"

Standland looked up from his deposit slip and set the
money decidedly down onto the desk.

"Well, I was hoping you could tell me." His tone held subdued irritation.

"I'm sorry?" Terrence fought to keep the worry from his voice.

"Well, I arrived this morning about an hour before the store was supposed to open, thankfully..." Standland began his story, "only to find a number of employees waiting outside the front door. I let them in and checked the schedule. I mean, I naturally assumed that the store manager was scheduled an hour and a half before opening-hour per regulations..."

He nodded in compliance, though he was aware that Larry very rarely ever showed up to work that early. In fact, Larry usually went out of his way to ignore or outright defy regulations any chance that he got. Still, he was surprised by his boss's audacity, considering Standland's presence.

"Right," Standland continued. "I waited for a few minutes, and then began assigning everyone their duties for the day. Once the store opened, I phoned Larry twice, but got no response. After the third time, I decided to take charge, and well....here we are."

Terrence shook his head in bewilderment. Sure, Larry would come and go as he pleased as long as Terrence was at the store. It was just a matter of course that he would pick up Larry's slack at any given moment. However, Larry's complete lack of concern over Standland being at the store, coupled with other recent developments, had Terrence convinced something sinister was going on.

"Well, I'm sure there's got to be a good reason." He felt compelled to say. "I mean, it's just not like Larry to be late like this."

Standland smiled broadly. Terrence wondered if Standland could read through his bullshit.

"Yes, I would assume so." Standland resumed counting the money before him.

Terrence nodded to close the conversation. He turned to exit the office, already planning a call to Larry's cellphone. He knew that Standland didn't have the number; he was pretty sure he wasn't even supposed to have it. When Larry vanished from work, he was determined to be out of touch.

"Oh," Standland's voice broke Terrence's thoughts. "There was another employee who didn't show up this morning."

Terrence turned back towards the desk.

"A new guy....ummm...." Standland searched the air for a name. "The older man."

Terrence felt a jump in his heartbeat. "Leonard? I mean, Mr. Best?"

"Yes! That's the one." Standland returned to the deposit. "Perhaps we need to find someone to replace him..."

Standland looked up to confirm with Terrence, however, all he saw was an empty doorway.

Chapter 34

The smell of barbecue sauce rose from the floor and drifted into Brad's nose. He stared at the mess he had just made, but wasn't really looking at it. He coughed back a lump in his throat and rubbed his damp eyes. He watched as a single drop fell to the puddle beneath him. Finally, he realized what he was doing and shook his head.

Absently, Brad reached for the basket behind him and pulled it to cover the mess. His shoes shuffled across the tiled floor towards the back; he passed customers and employees without a second glance. He didn't even bother to push the plastic curtain out of his way. Instead, he let it run across his face and fall behind him.

The cleaning supplies were at the far end, past the back stock of paper towels, napkins, foam cups, hygiene products, and paper plates. Brad found his way as his thoughts wandered; he entered the room and stood still. Here, amongst the wet mops and dust-filled brooms hanging from the walls, away from the rest of the store, Brad finally allowed himself to break down.

He thought of the years he had wasted on pills and pot. He thought of the night with Alex and the dancer he had drunkenly fucked. He thought of the bent wreckage that used to be his van, which was now sitting in a police impound somewhere. He thought of the man that he had seen with his wife, and he slammed his fist into the wall.

"Fuck!" Brad pulled his hand back and shook it. Instantly, it went limp and blood rushed to his knuckles. Pain shot through each finger and assailed his brain. A new well of tears flooded his eyes; he slumped against the wall and fell to the floor.

Feeling better than he had in weeks, he had awoken early that morning. He spent the time cleaning his house; he disposed of all paraphernalia and substances. He scrubbed away all hints of his useless past and planned for a sober future. With his house in order, Brad stepped into a hot shower. The scalding water washed away the dirt that clung to him. It absolved him of his sins and wrong-doings. It alleviated the pains left over from his wreck. He stepped onto the bathmat a new man, reborn.

He dressed himself in a uniform fresh out of the dryer and put on the new sneakers he had bought the night before. He stared at his reflection, proud of the man that stared back at him. He was neatly groomed, sharply dressed, and charged with purpose. This was the man his wife wanted, and it was time that she met him. Brad could barely feel the anxiety of withdrawal nipping at him as he waited for his taxi.

As he made small talk with the driver, he planned the meeting with his wife. It was still early, and she was probably just now getting up. He had stopped by the coffee shop and gotten her favorite latte and a muffin to surprise her with. He was a knight now, planning the courtship that would win him his true love.

He would start by wooing her with small trinkets and gifts, such as the coffee and breakfast. With each visit, he would prove to her that he was a changed man; one that was meant to make her happy. She would eventually learn to love him again, and once he had the $10,000, they would retire to their castle in the country side. He decided not to ruin his fantasy with thoughts on how he would actually have to accrue the money.

"Pull up right here." Brad smiled broadly to the driver. "I want to surprise her at the door."

The driver nodded politely, unimpressed with Brad's nobility.

As the taxi pulled up three houses down from the one his wife was staying at, Brad straightened his shirt. With coffee and muffin in hand, he stepped out of the cab and began his charge towards his wife's door. Before he could pass the first house, he saw the front door to her's open and another man step outside.

Brad stopped in his tracks as he stared at the man. He was tall, thin, and was dressed only in a white bath robe and slippers. He yawned as he strolled across the lawn towards the newspaper lying on the scorching sidewalk. Brad's eyes locked on the stranger as he turned and waved towards the door. Brad's heart sank as he saw his wife standing in the doorway, waving back. She quickly pulled the side of her own robe away to flash the man her breast. As they laughed and went back into the house, Brad threw the coffee to the ground and stomped on the muffin. He reentered the cab without a word and buried his head in his hands. Eventually, the cab driver pulled away and headed towards the store he had seen on Brad's name tag.

Cradling his broken hand, Brad screamed another obscenity. How could he have been so fucking stupid? He had never even thought to ask which "friend" his wife was staying with. He had never considered that she would leave him for another man. He had been so wrapped up in his own shit, that he had completely ignored her.

A wave of pain rattled the thoughts from his mind. His hand throbbed with each beat of his heart; he tried to focus on a solution. He had no insurance to visit the doctor, and he wasn't going to explain to Larry how he'd hurt his hand. Suddenly, a dim light shined from the back of his mind. Brad pulled himself to his feet and took a deep breath. He gently slid his bleeding hand into his pocket, wincing from the pain brought by the brief contact. With his good hand, he wiped the sweat from his forehead and made his way down to the other end of the back room.

Once again, he avoided the employees scurrying around and eventually made it to the break area. He peered into the drab room; several employees ate as courtroom television blared from the television set. He kept his wits and focused on the lockers at the opposite side of the room. He trotted past the lopsided tables and the employees sitting at them. The chubby cashier shoved a hot dog in her mouth and recounted the latest episode of her soap opera to a bored stocker.

Brad turned the dial on the combination lock and pulled it down. He opened the door to his locker and prayed for a miracle. He stuck his good hand in and moved it around. When he pulled it back out, he held a crumbled plastic bag with two small pills tucked inside. He quickly popped them into his mouth and swallowed. He hoped they were the painkillers that he thought they were.

As he made his way back to the mop room, a warm calm flowed over his body. The pain in his hand gradually subsided, and peace came into his mind. He grabbed the mop he'd originally come back there for and headed to clean up the barbecue sauce. He replayed the events of the morning through his mind once more. This time, his wife's actions were less spiteful and more desperate. He realized that she hadn't gone to another man to hurt him. In fact, Brad now saw that he had driven her away and this vulture had picked her up.

Brad reshaped his wife into an innocent victim. She was a babe lost to the wilderness only to be gobbled up by a lone wolf. How dare this man take advantage of her while she was in such a fragile state! As he mopped up the mixture of glass and sauce, Brad dreamed of himself as a knight once more. He would dash in on his mighty steed and rescue his wife from her evil captor. He would prove his love and take her to the castle in the country. All he needed was Excalibur at his side. He sloshed the mop across the stained tile once more and envisioned the $10,000 that would be served up to him by the Lady of the Lake....or yanked from the stone....

Brad's thoughts began to cloud as the full effect of the pills set in. For the next thirty minutes, he swirled the mop and tried to focus on a plan to steal the prize money that would be given away in one week.

Chapter 35

Terrence pulled his car up to the front of Leonard Best's apartment building. It had been years since he had been in this neighborhood. Some of the names on the buildings had changed, and one or two had disappeared, but he recognized his old stomping grounds instantly.

As he kept one eye out on the street, Terrence glanced down at the scrap piece of paper in his hand. On it was Leonard's address and apartment number that Terrence had taken from a file at work. He had convinced Standland to let him take the deposit to the bank and said that he would stop and grab them both lunch as well. That had been nearly an hour ago, but Terrence wasn't worried. Not about Standland, anyway.

After several unsuccessful rings at the buzzer near the building's entrance, he tried the door handle. He was not surprised that it opened without as much as a tug. Everything in this part of town was broken and had been for a number of years. The streets had potholes; the buildings were falling apart. Even the residents seemed disheartened and worn out. That's what concerned Terrence the most. He was all too familiar with how dangerous those types of people could be.

He climbed the steps to the third floor of the apartment building. He checked his paper again and found the correct door. At first, he knocked lightly. When there was no response, he knocked louder. He had begun pounding on the door when a neighbor, a black woman in her late sixties, opened the door across the hall and poked her head out.

"What are you banging on Mr. Best's door like that for?" her tone was scolding, like a grandmother rebuking a young child.

"I'm sorry if I bothered you," Terrence took a step towards the woman's door. She instinctively pulled it closer, leaving only a sliver of open space. "I'm looking for Mr. Best.

I'm his boss over at the MegaSaver. Do you know where I can find him?"

"His boss, huh?" The woman's skepticism poured through the crack of the doorway. "Well, he ain't home."

"Can you please tell me where he is?" Terrence was growing frustrated and nervous. He was having a hard time controlling his anger. "He didn't show up for his shift today, and I was worried about him."

The woman's eyes softened, and she opened the door slightly. Her expression was one of sadness and penance.

"I'm sorry to tell you that Mr. Best is in the hospital." Her words were gentle.

"What happened? Is he alright?" Terrence could feel his breath catch at the news.

"I don't know. I just heard that they found him out on the sidewalk last night." The woman stepped fully into the hallway. She was dressed in a baggy rag of a shirt and threadbare pants that were at least thirty years old.

Terrence looked down at the floor to compose himself. He had not expected to react in such a way.

"It seems like he may have fainted or had a heart attack." The woman shook her head. "Or, maybe those little hoodlum kids jumped him. It wouldn't be the first time that's happened around here."

Terrence thanked the woman for her time and got the name of the hospital Leonard had been taken to. He rocketed down the stairs of the apartment building and jumped into his car. Lunch with Standland would have to wait. He put the car in gear and headed towards the hospital.

Chapter 36

Larry fanned himself as he entered the MegaSaver. The seventy-five degree air did little to relieve his flushed face. His shirt was already damp from sweat, and his head was throbbing. He marched up to the thermostat, and jammed his fingers into the buttons. Above his head, the compressors whined as they were forced to life. Cool air trickled from the ceiling vents as the sound of metal scraping metal echoed throughout the store. Almost instantly, Michael Standland stormed out of the office.

"Who is messing with the thermo…" Standland's words hit the brick wall of Larry's crimson death stare. "Larry, it's nice of you to join us this morning."

"I'm on the schedule, aren't I?" He was having a bad enough day already and was in no mood for this hairless freak.

"Yes, actually, you are." Standland's tone was verging on antagonistic. "Or, rather, you were four hours ago."

"Yeah, well, I had shit to do." Larry brushed past Standland and headed up to his office. He wasn't going to explain himself to anyone from home office.

"Larry, we need to talk," Standland followed him up the stairs, letting each step pound louder than he normally would have. "We have got to get the store ready for the arrival of the prize money. I've hired a security guard and would like…."

Larry entered his office without acknowledging Standland's comments.

"Larry? Are you listening to me?" Standland reached out and firmly grasped his shoulder. Larry had had enough.

"No, asshole, I'm not." Larry spun to face Standland. "I don't really give a shit what you want to talk about. I don't really care what you think of me, or how you think I should run my store."

Standland released his grasp and took a step back. His face was instantly filled with disbelief. Larry seized the moment.

"I get that you are some big shit hot shot in the rest of the company, and that you are gonna have your little sale here and then you'll go away," Larry licked his dry lips. "And that's exactly what I'm waiting for: for you to go away."

Dumb-stricken, Standland moved his lips without speaking. Larry leaned in closer.

"So, why don't you go hang some signs or suck some ad guy's dick or something, and let me do my fucking job?" Larry turned back to his desk in triumph.

"I..I.." the hairless man stammered, "I could have your job."

Larry reached into his desk drawer, pulled out his bottle of whiskey and poured himself a shot. He made direct eye contact with Standland as he drank it in one gulp.

"Go for it, hot shot." Larry slammed the glass down and pointed towards the office door.

Standland tucked his tail between his legs and bolted to the sales floor. The ache in Larry's head subsided, and he stared down at the registers. Where was Maxine when he needed her?

Chapter 37

The automatic doors opened too slowly for Terrence; he grabbed them and forced them apart as he barreled through the entryway. His pace was faster than he expected, and his worry greater than he would have anticipated. For reasons that were all his own, Terrence felt a connection to the old man he had recently hired at the MegaSaver. That connection now brought him to the front desk of the hospital Leonard was brought to the night before.

"Excuse me..." Terrence tried to interrupt the nurse's phone conversation. A flash of warning from her eyes cut him off. He leaned away from the counter as she continued her conversation.

"I'm not seeing it....wait....no..." The nurse's fingers danced around her keyboard as her eyes scanned the computer screen. Minutes ticked by as she attempted to fill in missing data on a patient's insurance form over the phone. Terrence struggled to keep his anger in check; he forced his breath in and out at regular intervals. Finally, the nurse hung up and acknowledged him.

"Yes, sir?" The nurse did her best bank teller impersonation. No trace of emotion and only the slightest hint of impatience rounded her words.

"Yes, ma'am." Terrence steadied his tone as best he could. "I'm looking for the room number of a patient, Mr. Leonard Best. He was brought in last night."

"One moment..." The nurse's eyes returned to her computer screen and her fingers began flying across the keys again. "Yes, sir. He's in room number nine on the third floor."

The nurse briefly glanced up to make eye contact with Terrence, though she was met only by the back of his head. Without comment, she answered her ringing phone and began punching her keyboard again.

Terrence strode down the hallway on the third floor. The elevator had dropped him off in the middle of the corridor; Leonard's room was all the way at the other end. He wondered what he would say to the old man when he reached him. What kind of shape would he be in? Terrence thought of tubes and beeping heart monitors and stopped in his tracks. He wasn't sure he was prepared to see something like that.

After taking a few more steps, he found the plaque that marked Leonard's room. He looked down at his feet, took a deep breath, and stared through the small window in the top of the door. There, he could see Leonard lying in bed with his eyes closed; his chest slowly moved up and down. From where he was standing, Terrence could see a large bruise on the side of Leonard's face and several scratches on his forehead. His right hand was wrapped in gauze, and there were several bandages along his arms.

"Excuse me," a voice behind him made Terrence turn quickly.

"Yes?" He was facing another nurse, this time a younger woman in her mid-twenties. She was dressed in blue-green scrubs and held a clipboard. Her eyes were wide; there was only a faint hint of intellect behind them.

"Are you Thomas Best?" the nurse's voice was hopeful. "Are you Mr. Best's son?"

"Yes, I am." Terrence smiled faintly and returned his stare towards the window in the door. He hoped she bought it.

"Oh, good!" The nurse smiled broadly to herself and checked something on her clipboard. "We've been trying to reach you for the past several hours."

"How is he?" Terrence brushed aside the nurse's unasked question.

"Well," the nurse consulted her clipboard again, "his breathing has stabilized, and we've cleaned his wounds. We gave him something to help him sleep while we treat the asthma and diabetes."

Terrence turned to face the nurse again. He searched his memory for any instance of seeing Leonard using insulin or an inhaler. Though he didn't keep especially close tabs on the man, he couldn't recall him using either.

"Diabetes? Asthma?" He kept his voice even.

"Yes, sir. His blood sugar levels were off, and his breathing was labored when he was brought in. Judging by his condition, it's likely that he wasn't even aware of having them." He could tell she was using the most consoling voice she could muster.

"Is he going to be alright?" Terrence held his breath.

"I believe so," she flipped pages in Leonard's chart. "They sure did one hell of a number on the poor guy."

"So, he was attacked?" His voice cracked, surprising himself.

"Yes, sir. Didn't you get the messages I left? About the neighbor calling 911?" the nurse's wide eyes reflected the fluorescent lights in the ceiling.

"When do you expect to release him?" He kept his eyes locked on Leonard's face.

"Not for a few days. We need to get his blood sugar under control and give his knee a rest." Terrence shot the nurse a surprised look which sent her back to her clipboard. "Oh, I'm sorry. I forgot to mention his sprained knee."

As the nurse slowly withdrew herself from the conversation and made her way to the next patient, he took a deep breath. He realized that Leonard had little hope of returning to work anytime soon, if at all. He glanced at his watch and noticed he'd been gone from the MegaSaver for over two hours. He cursed himself and made his way back down the corridor to the elevator. He knew tonight would be a sleepless one; however, it would be filled with more than aimless driving.

Chapter 38

Larry leaned back in his desk chair with his arms raised above his head. His face was lifted towards the ceiling, though his eyes were closed. His headache had left him, although his wife's pitiful words still rang in his mind. She had woken him up at five am by throwing their checkbook at his head. Larry, eyes bloodshot and throat dry, didn't comprehend (or even hear) the first few sentences of his wife's hysterics. Lack of sleep and abundance of whiskey provoked an unruly response from his lips.

"What the fuck are you yapping about?" Larry stared daggers at his wife. "I'm trying to fucking sleep for Christ's sake!"

"You haven't listened to a word I've said, have you?" Cynthia's eyes were wet with tears, her voice bordered on frenzy.

"No, Goddamit. I just told you I was trying to sleep." He laid his head back down on his pillow in a futile attempt to dismiss his wife's concerns.

"Larry!" her voice was shrill and high-pitched, like a helium balloon being slowly drained, "Wake up and listen to me!"

"WHAT?!" He jerked the covers from his body, throwing them to the floor. He turned over and sat up, facing his delirious wife, and folded his arms. He had had enough of her whining, and figured this would be the fastest way to press through it and get back to sleep. Cynthia took a step back in fear, and her voice softened.

"I was trying to tell you that something's wrong with our checking account." Her voice was sheepish and chastened.

Larry's anger suddenly gave way to fear, and his eyes focused. His throat was barren, and he coughed to loosen his words. He took a step out of bed and headed towards the bathroom for a cup of water. He hoped that he looked as nonchalant as he was attempting to.

"What do you mean?" Larry filled a small glass with cold water and chugged it.

"Well, I went to pay the car note the other day," Cynthia had regained some confidence as she noticed her husband's interest, "and they declined the check."

"Why would they do that?" Larry filled the glass a second time and gulped down the water. Fuck, this wasn't a conversation he wanted to ever have; much less three hours after passing out drunk.

"I thought there was something wrong with the check reader, so I went to the bank.."

"What the fuck for?" he turned and stared at her.

"Um, to see how much money we had in the account." Cynthia's eyes were wide and confused.

Larry grunted.

"Anyways, I talked to the lady at the bank, and she said that there had been several large withdrawals from the account over the past two weeks or so. " Cynthia's voice had grown cautionary.

"For how much?" He attempted to act as angry and shocked as she would expect him to. He wasn't sure he was pulling it off.

"A few hundred dollars," Cynthia spoke as if she were passing on the latest gossip. "Do you think someone could have stolen one of our ATM cards or something?"

Inspired by his wife's suggestion, he swallowed another glass of water and set it down with determination. He turned to face her and forced a rush of blood to his face. By God, she was going to get the performance of his life.

"You're Goddamn right that's what happened!" Anger rang from each word Larry spoke.

"Really?" Cynthia replied with a mix of both fear and hope.

"I told you about buying all that shit online from epay or spacebook, or whatever the hell you look at." He stomped out of the bathroom towards the kitchen to make coffee.

"Honey!" Cynthia reacted like a chastised child. "You know I haven't been on there in months. Ever since you told me to stop."

"Bullshit!" Larry took a blind shot. "I can see all the shit you buy online every time you buy it!"

Cynthia stopped in her tracks. She knew she had been caught and was now facing punishment for her actions. Tears began to well in her eyes.

"I'm sorry, honey. I promise I'll never do it again."

Larry turned and looked at his weeping wife. A wave of pity ran through him for a split second. He thought about the affair he was having with Maxine and how much it could hurt the woman in front of him. He had to admit that he had never been especially fond of his wife; he had married her more out of a sense of responsibility and a fear of child support. Yet, there were times when he did enjoy her company and occasionally connected with her as a person. Her entire life was supported by Larry; she was the mother of his child and the keeper of his home. She didn't deserve to have a breakdown at five thirty in the morning.

"Look, it's okay." He took a step towards her and took her hand. "I'll go by the bank later and take care of everything, ok?"

Relief flooded Cynthia's face, and she smiled. She grabbed Larry and wrapped her arms around him. She hugged him tightly against her body, and Larry awkwardly returned the embrace.

"Thank you so much, Larry." Cynthia's tears were now of joy. "You really are a good man, do you know it?"

He stiffly rubbed his wife's back with his hand. "Sure, baby. I know."

A wave of euphoria rushed over Larry as he sat in his office chair. His eyes clenched; his body tightened. His breath spiked, and he exhaled deeply as fluid rushed from his body. Completely relaxed, he leaned back in his chair and smiled.

"Holy fuck, that's just what I needed…" Larry looked down towards his crotch. "Thank you."

"No problem, sweetheart." Maxine raised herself off her knees and helped him zip his pants back up. She grabbed a tissue from the dispenser on his desk and wiped her lips. She grabbed her whiskey drink and swallowed it; rinsing in the process.

"Listen, darling," Maxine turned up the sugar coat on her drawl, "I don't mean to be asking favors, but my phone bill's due tomorrow, and I could sure use a little help."

He buckled his belt and looked at Maxine. Here it was. The moment of truth had arrived. Larry took a deep breath and contemplated his next move.

"Listen, Maxie. We need to talk."

Chapter 39

Yellow streetlights shone down on the crumbling buildings of Leonard Best's neighborhood. The stench of sweat and desperation tainted the air; the loud thumping sounds of car stereos and the occasional gun shot broke the quiet stillness of the streets. There were only a few people milling outside of their homes, but most walked quickly and quietly; their heads down and their eyes peeled for any sign of danger. As Terrence drove along slowly, he too kept his eyes alert.

He had made another trip to the hospital after work only to be told that visiting hours were over. He argued with a few nurses, most of which seemed sympathetic, but still unable to comply with his wishes. After finally getting through to the last nurse, he was allowed five minutes to check on Leonard. He spent those minutes watching the man sleep soundly as his IV dripped and heart monitors beeped steadily. Leonard's condition seemed a bit improved, according to the nurses Terrence spoke to. They were even optimistic of an early discharge. Terrence couldn't help but wonder, though, which had more to do with that: Leonard's condition or his insurance status.

After leaving the hospital, Terrence felt a familiar worry take hold in his mind. He knew sleep would be a long way off; he sought refuge in his vehicle and decided to take the long way home. Soon, he found himself back in the old neighborhood. His car crept along the empty streets like a shark prowling still waters.

He rounded the corner and pulled up to the curb; he turned his engine off, and sat in the darkness. Straight ahead of him stood the bus stop that Leonard had gotten off at the night before. Just a few yards away was the park he was found lying next to. Terrence perused the buildings around him. Most of the windows had lights shining behind them; he watched as some of them began to go out. Once the majority had been extinguished, Terrence leaned back in his seat and began watching the park.

For a while, Terrence saw nothing. The streets had become almost completely vacant. There were no buses running, no taxis pulling up. The park was especially still in the darkness. There were no children playing on the jungle gym. There were no people jogging or walking around the paths. Even the swings stood motionless in the hot, breezeless night.

Terrence sat in his car, twirling an old knife around in his hands. His face burned with anger. Part of his mind told him to just put the car in gear and head home to his wife. The other kept replaying the image of Leonard being beaten and kicked into the ground. He pictured the old man gasping for air and yelling for help as some young thug punched him again, and again.

The sound of voices echoing in the park broke Terrence's concentration. He turned to see a group of shadowy figures in the distance. From the jumbled voices and clumsy laughter, he could tell the figures must be young. A flash from a cigarette lighter illuminated their faces just long enough to confirm his suspicions. He watched as the teens smoked and drank; they told lewd jokes and occasionally pushed each other around.

Terrence stared at the young men; he sized them up and quickly determined each of their weaknesses. He could easily take three of them at once. The other two might present a problem.

"Hey, man. Hey! Watch this shit!" one of the teenagers threw himself to the ground and clutched his chest. The others encircled him and pretended to kick. The boy on the ground laughed and made the sounds of a crying baby. Terrence's sudden, tight grip on the knife turned his knuckles a darker shade of black. The group cracked up; the young men pushed each other and clapped their hands. They were so proud of what they had done. Terrence threw his car door open and launched himself toward the teenagers.

149

Chapter 40

"I don't understand what you're saying to me." Maxine stared at Larry's flushed face as he stammered.

Dammit. Larry stood up from his desk. He was never good at these kinds of things, which is probably how he ended up married in the first place. He took a deep breath and decided to try again.

"Listen, Maxine. It's not that I'm unhappy with you or anything, but…" Larry swallowed hard at the lump in his throat.

"But, what?" Maxine's stare could cut through a wall of steel.

"It's…my wife. She's started to question me about things." Larry only hoped he'd said enough to satisfy Maxine's questions.

"What kinds of things?" She was determined to nail him down.

Goddammit. Larry paced back and forth. He ran his fingers over his smooth head and breathed heavily. He had tangled himself in a web that he was finding extremely difficult to cut his way out of.

"What kinds of things do you think? She's asking why I'm staying at work so late all the time; why I'm not paying her any attention…." Larry lied.

Maxine stared at him without saying a word. The weight of the world began pressing down on his chest. Her eyes drove him further and further into a corner. He coughed and licked his lips as he waited for her to speak. She did not. He could feel his blood begin to boil; he decided to release the pressure before he exploded.

"Goddammit! It's the money, okay?" Larry had never felt so defeated and vulnerable before.

"I see." Maxine continued staring at Larry. Her eyes betrayed no feelings of any type, and her words were shielded with ice.

Larry walked over to Maxine and began to plead his case.

"Dammit, Maxie. Don't you understand?" He begged. "I can't keep pulling money out of my account or shorting my deposit."

Still nothing.

"My wife started rummaging around our checking account the other day, and I can't explain to her where it's all going!" He laid his sob story on thick. "And then this asshole Standland starts sticking his fucking nose into the store's....MY store's money."

Not a word.

"It's just getting to be too much, Maxie!" Larry stood close to Maxine, hoping to either intimidate or ingratiate himself to her. "Don't you understand?"

Maxine had had enough.

"Do you know what I understand, you little asshole?" Maxine's voice was not loud. It was sharp and solid, commanding the entire room without volume. "I understand that my boss made sexual advances towards me with the promise of a raise and a promotion."

She took a step forward, and Larry backed up.

"I understand that my boss has been taking me to trashy hotels and forcing himself on me in order to satisfy some perverted need to control my black skin."

They took another step.

"I understand that my store manager is unable to help out his employee when she's having a hard time with money, but is clearly capable of helping himself to some of her pussy, whenever he feels like it."

One more step.

"I understand that he has, on occasion, taken money from the store's deposit violating both company policy and the law."

Maxine seemed to grow an inch in height with every word she spoke.

"I understand that the man in front of me repeatedly desecrated the vows of his marriage both on company property and outside of it."

Larry shrunk into a ball.

"And, I completely understand that not one minute after shooting his load into my mouth, this slimy son of a bitch decided I wasn't good enough to swallow it."

Tears welled in both of their eyes.

"Is that about right, or have I misunderstood something?" Maxine challenged Larry as he nearly tripped on something behind him.

He leaned against his desk, having become physically afraid of Maxine's outrage. His voice was barely audible as he spoke.

"What did you say, asshole?" Maxine leaned forward.

Larry licked his lips and tried again. "I said....What are you going to do to me?"

Maxine's laugh was sudden and jarring. It erupted with an unsettling force and vigor; she stepped back from Larry to give him breathing room.

"I don't know, Larry." She chuckled. "I suppose my first instinct would be to call your wife and let her know what's been going on."

He flinched at the thought of the costly divorce that would lie ahead of him. He'd end up living in some tiny apartment in some shitty part of town just so he could afford child support and alimony. Hell, he may even end up living in the King's Hotel room that he and Maxie had shared so often.

"Or, maybe I should talk to Michael Standland tomorrow." Maxine threw his name like a grenade into Larry's foxhole. "I'm sure he'd be very interested in his missing deposit money and the lurid ways you've been spending it!"

Larry could almost feel the cold, steel bars of his cell pressing against his hands. He imagined the thin mattress of the cot he'd be forced to sleep on, and the gang members, drug dealers, rapists, and murderers that would become his new neighbors. Larry shuddered at the sound of his own, uncontrollable yelp.

"Maybe, I should even get a lawyer," Maxine pondered aloud. "You know, one of those white men from TV that's always talking about sexual harassment. That way, I could get your wife to leave you, your ass thrown in jail, and a big lawsuit settlement out of it."

Visions of destitution and imprisonment shuffled through Larry's mind. How could he have been so stupid? He should have known that this would only end badly. What the hell did he think was going to happen? Did he think that they would one day come to a nice, neat mutual agreement to end the affair? How had he been so fucking stupid enough to throw away his career, his house, his marriage all for a piece of ass? Goddamit.

"But, you know what? I don't think that's what I'm gonna do." Maxine returned her gaze to Larry's curled figure.

Larry uncovered his head and looked towards her. "No?"

"No, Larry." She met his eyes and held them.

"Why not?" Larry was gun shy, but puzzled.

"Because, in the long run, I need you Larry." Maxine's tone softened just slightly.

"What?" Larry had uncurled from his fetal position.

"There's something I need you to understand, Larry." Maxine made direct eye contact. "I'm pregnant with your baby."

Chapter 41

The warm vodka stung Brad's lips as he sipped the pint bottle in the grizzly air. His battered body ached with each movement; his stomach cramped from hunger and dehydration. With each drink, he felt the pain less and less, though, emotionally, he was breaking apart.

He stood across the street, staring at the house his wife was shacking up in. Neighbors had passed him, throwing concerned looks in his direction, but he hadn't cared. All he could think about was her. He envisioned them lying out in the sun, basking in the sobering warmth as it reflected from the pristine pool at Cooling Meadows. He felt her skin next to his. He tasted the softness of her lips and the gentleness of her touch. He took another drink.

There were only two things standing in their way. First, was the money problem. He was already formulating a plan for that one. Within days, it would be his. The other obstacle was the asshole across the street. Brad knew he had to get that man out of the picture before his wife would even consider going to the resort with him. He chugged the remaining alcohol and stumbled towards the house.

Brad's finger pressed the doorbell and held it in position. He could hear the chime ring over and over again inside. Angry yells were muffled by the walls of the house, but loud enough to let Brad know the man was storming towards the door. He pulled his right leg back in an offensive stance and prepared for battle.

"Yeah, what the fuck do you want?" the front door had flown open, revealing an angry, half-dressed man.

"I...want...my wife...back." Brad forced the words out. The vodka and heat had caused his stomach to become unsettled.

"I'm sorry. Who the hell are you?" the man eyed him with amused pity.

"I...want...my wife...back," Brad blinked his eyes. Maybe he hadn't spoken the first time.

"Listen, buddy. I'm right in the middle of something," the man smirked. "Why don't you just take yourself home and sober up?"

Brad lifted his hand and stabbed his fingers into the man's bare chest.

"Why don't you...just...go...shit?" He cocked his eyebrow in defiance.

"Brad?" his wife poked her head through the door frame. She was wearing a robe, and her hair was disheveled, "What the hell are you doing here?"

He lifted his eyes to meet hers. He smiled towards her, but it was not returned.

"Oh! So you're *Brad*?" the man made a mockery of his name. "You're the asshole who broke this beautiful woman's heart!"

Brad's eyes jolted from his wife to the man. He could feel the anger churning within him. It cut through the thick haze of alcohol and self-loathing.

"God, I thought I'd never get to meet you!" the man continued his performance, "I always wondered what kind of sad son of a bitch could drive a woman like this from his bed to mine."

She lowered her eyes in a flicker of shame and embarrassment.

"You should go home, Brad," her tone was kinder than it had been in years.

The man leaned in close to Brad's face.

"I shouldn't complain. I mean, buddy, she is fantastic in the sack." The man laughed cruelly and turned to make sure she was just as amused.

Glass exploded across the man's face as the empty vodka bottle tore into his skin. Blood gushed onto the ground and the man fell over, stunned. She screamed and dropped to her knees.

155

"What the fuck is wrong with you?" she yelled at Brad, before turning to help the man who lay groaning at her side.

Brad stared at the two for a moment before speaking. Was that his bottle that ripped into the guy's head? Had he been the one to move his arm? He was alarmed by the feeling that he was no longer in control of his actions.

He looked at the piece of glass he was holding and dropped it. He raised his arms out towards his wife and her bleeding lover to help them.

"Get the fuck out of here, you psychotic son of a bitch!" Her eyes burned with fear and hatred.

The man coughed up shards and crawled into the house.

"I'm calling the fucking cops!" the man reached for a phone that was somewhere in the living room.

Brad's eyes teared as he took a step back from the door. He was as helpless as a wounded animal. He ran into the humid darkness; weeping for the future he had probably just destroyed.

Chapter 42

When he had gotten the phone call announcing his wife's labor, Larry had been in the middle of a conference with one of his District Managers. Sitting across the desk from him, Larry stared at the back pages of a financial report his boss was silently reading. Nicholas Edwards, District Manager of Operations for Food Lot, Inc, dissected each report as if he were divining Larry's future. He had said very little as Larry had entered the room, sat down in the chair, and asked what the meeting was about. Instead, Edwards poured over each figure with a scalpel of forecasts and projections; leaving Larry to awkwardly shift back and forth. Finally, he spoke.

"Larry, I'm seeing a problem here." Edwards' words were short and condescending.

"What are you talking about?" Larry returned the tone with a side of resentment.

"Well, I see that your overall sales have steadily decreased over the last fiscal year." Edwards let the information hang in the air.

"Well, I think that's because of the housing market and..." Larry attempted to plead his case to the back of the papers.

"Now, what I find interesting," Edwards continued as if Larry had never spoken, "is that your payroll hours have remained consistent and sometimes even increased over this same time frame."

Larry felt a rush of heat flow to his face and a glob of sweat form at his brow. His teeth began to grind into each other, and he took quick, short breaths. How dare this asshole cut him off!

"Yes, sir. As I was saying..." Larry's calm was bucking wildly against his anger.

"So, I gotta ask," the papers lowered, finally revealing Edwards' face to Larry, "why wouldn't you cut hours or lay off

157

some people? I mean, I see here that you hired two cashiers in February right after the holiday rush!"

The rage had finally reached critical mass within Larry. He didn't have time to sit in his own office, across his own desk, in his own store, and be chastised by some corporate suit about the way he ran his business. If it wasn't for him, they wouldn't have the goddamn store in the first place.

"Alright, you listen to me…" Larry leaned over the edge of his desk towards Edwards. The other man held his hands in a triangle at his mouth and stared back intently.

Before Larry could proceed with his insubordinate outburst, the phone beside Edwards rang. Edwards' hand was just beginning to move towards the receiver as Larry snatched it up. Larry's eyes dared the other man to confront him. He did not.

"Yes." Larry's tone transformed the greeting to a demand. "What? Now? This is really not a good time."

Larry slammed the receiver down and turned towards the door.

"Excuse me, Larry." Edwards's eyes widened in exasperation. "Where are you going? We're not done here."

"My wife's having a fucking baby." Larry yelled without a glance backwards.

Larry stormed out of the office and flew down the stairs, leaving Edwards alone with his reports. Unable to think of another way to handle the situation, Edwards packed the paperwork into his briefcase and left for the day.

As Larry drove across town towards the hospital, his cell phone rang. He flipped it open in irritation and barked another "Hello?" He glanced up just in time to see that a light was turning red in front of him. He slammed on his breaks, which squealed as his tires dragged across the black concrete.

"What the fuck are you talking about?" Larry berated his wife over the phone. "I just rushed out of a very important meeting with a guy from corporate because I thought you were having a baby."

The light changed to green, and yet Larry sat still.

158

"False labor? What the hell is that?" A car horn shrieked behind him, and Larry stepped on the gas. (Only after flipping the other driver off, of course.)

"So when the hell do they think you're gonna have the damn thing?" Larry kept his route, not knowing what exactly was happening. "Some time today? That's the best you can do? Not an hour from now, or around dinner, or maybe just before midnight?"

He had always hated waiting for other people. If an interviewee showed up even one minute late, Larry canceled the interview. If a vendor was running behind for a meeting, he refused to purchase their product. Even when he answered the phone, he said hello and waited exactly one second; if no reply was heard, he immediately slammed down the phone. He refused to be kept waiting for the birth of his child, especially, by the kid itself.

"Fine. I'm gonna stop off and get something to eat. Call me when it's about to happen." Larry flipped the phone closed and tossed it into the passenger seat. He turned the car around and began heading back towards the store.

As he drove, he thought of the conversation that awaited him and grunted. Fuck this. He wasn't going back to that fucking corporate asshole and his meeting. Larry abruptly shifted lanes and pulled off towards the interstate. After a short drive, he took his normal parking spot and sauntered up to the bar of the Platinum Pony.

The first couple of drinks, he told himself, were to calm his nerves after his meeting. The ones after that were to allay his fears of becoming a father. After a couple of hours, the drinks began to fuel a vilification of his wife and her desire to ruin and entrap him with the creature she was about to give birth to.

By early evening, Larry's phone began to ring with news from his wife. Instead of answering and running off to the hospital, he threw it onto the bar and yelled obscenities which he hoped would travel to the beast in his wife's womb. He even began to order shots for himself and some of the women to take each time his phone rang. After the third shot, one of the dancers dragged Larry to a waiting cab and sent him on his way to the hospital.

By the time he arrived, he was nauseous and nearly comatose. The driver pulled Larry from his cab and shoved him towards the hospital entrance. As he stumbled down the hallways, Larry bumped into several nurses and attempted to ask them for directions to his wife's room. The combination of his belligerent attitude, and the slurring of his words, made it difficult for him to find anyone willing or able to help him. He was finally led to his room by one of the nurses just in time to see his daughter's head begin to make its way out.

The room was full of parents and other relatives; the barrage of camera flashes made Larry uneasy on his feet. As Cynthia shrieked in pain, the doctor began yelling his instructions. Eventually, the entire room erupted in a chant of "Push! Push! Push!" Finally, the shrill sounds of a crying baby were heard, and Larry was promptly hauled over to his wife's side.

"Isn't she beautiful?" Cynthia rubbed Larry's arm as the baby was wrapped in a blanket.

Larry mumbled something incoherent.

"Would you like to hold her?" The doctor turned and presented Larry with his first born. There, wrapped in a pink blanket, lay a screaming, wrinkled child. She was still wet with her mother's juices, and the freshly cut umbilical chord dangled at her stomach. Larry began to quiver and had to look away from the baby. Out of the corner of his eye, he saw the nurse remove the afterbirth from his wife's vagina. Larry immediately unleashed a river of vomit from his mouth and fell face first to the floor.

As he lay on the cold tile, hovering near coherence, Larry could hear remarks of disgust coming from all around him. He could distinctly make out his wife's weeping sounds, and the censures of her father. Nurses checked his vitals, and the doctor questioned his well-being. The voices gradually blurred together until they were indistinguishable. Soon, however, Larry began to hear one voice rise from the background. It was harsh and resentful, and shot through all the murmurs surrounding it.

"Get your ridiculous ass up!"

Larry blinked his eyes until the image in front of him came into focus. He could make out the leg to the couch in his office. Confused, he pushed his arms against the floor and looked around. Maxine stood above him, her eyes stabbing him through the heart.

"What happened?" Larry sat up and attempted to shake off the queasy feeling in his stomach.

"You fainted, asshole." Maxine resisted the urge to kick him in the face.

"Oh." Embarrassed, Larry got to his feet. He still felt uneasy, though pride kept him standing.

"So, you ain't got anything else to say?" Maxine tapped her foot impatiently.

"I....I just don't understand...how.' It was the only thing that came to Larry's mind.

"Unbelievable!" Maxine stormed out of the office.

"Wait!" Larry followed her down the steps.

As they reached the bottom of the stairs, Larry reached out and grabbed Maxine's shoulder. She refused to stop until she got to the door.

"Maxine, for God's sake wait." He tightened his grip.

"Open the door, Larry." she refused to face him.

"Can we talk about this for a minute?" He pleaded.

"What's there to talk about?" Maxine spun around with a fury.

"What do you mean, what's there to talk about?" Larry's eyes were wide and filled with terror. "We've got to decide what to do about this."

"You mean what you're going to do about this." Maxine took a step towards Larry. "I suggest you start thinking up names."

"What? You don't mean you're actually gonna have this thing, do you?" The thought had never occurred to him that he would become a father again.

'THING? This THING?" Maxine's voice echoed throughout the entire empty store. "This *thing* is going to be your child, Larry. Get used to it."

"You can't be serious! I can't have another kid." He was bewildered. "You can't have a kid at your age!"

"If you weren't the father of my child, I would kick you in your dick right now." Maxine reared her leg back.

Instinctively, Larry covered his crotch.

"Listen," he began, "what I meant was that it would be dangerous for you to have a kid at your age. I'm thinking about your well-being, too."

"Bullshit! You've been thinking about yourself from moment number one." Maxine was furious. "All you've ever thought about is yourself. How much money you could bonus by keeping my pay low. How much you wanna get your dick sucked or how good it would feel to get laid. You never cared about who was on the other end. And now, it's time to pay the price for your selfishness."

Larry stood with his head down staring at his shoes. The air was heavy with resentment and truth. He felt as if he were standing in a pit with dirt falling down on top of him from all sides. His breath became short and rapid. His vision was tunneling again. His only thought: I have to escape.

"Well, Maxie….." his voice was barely audible, "if it's about the money…"

"What!?!" Maxine was outraged. "Are you offering me money to kill our baby? Is that what you're telling me?"

"Come on, Maxine!" Larry was exasperated. "You know it would be the best thing. You'd get something out of it; I'd get something out of it. Think about my daughter and my wife."

Larry, feeling a sliver of optimism, took at step towards her. He pulled out his check book from his back pocket and scribbled it out. He handed the check to Maxine with a shaking hand. She stared at it without a word.

"Come on, you know it's the right thing to do. Just give me a couple of days to get the money shifted around into the account. Then, we can take care of this little problem." Larry shifted to his most reassuring tone.

"Five hundred dollars?" Maxine jerked her head up towards Larry. "Five hundred fucking dollars!"

She ripped the check up and threw it into his face. He leapt backwards in terror.

"You listen to me, you stupid son of a bitch." Maxine pointed her painted fingernail into Larry's face. "I'm having your baby, and there's no amount of money you can pay me to weasel your way out of it."

She abruptly turned and stormed out of the front door. Larry stood in silent shock for a few moments. The sound of Maxine's revving engine finally broke his trance. He rushed out of the door towards her car.

"Maxie, wait! Come on, we can work something out!" Larry yelled as her car peeled out of the parking lot. As it quickly made its way out of sight, his voice got louder and louder. "Maxine! Maxine!"

Tears flowed from his eyes, and he finally accepted defeat. He covered his face and squatted down in the deserted parking lot. He cried for God's help. He cursed God for putting him in this situation. He begged for a miscarriage. He blamed himself. He blamed Maxine. He wept for the divorce he knew was coming as he buried his face into his hands. He never heard the footsteps behind him, or felt the blow to the back of his head.

Chapter 43

The first kid was instantly knocked to the ground. His nose broke before he was even able to comprehend what was happening. The second teen managed to throw one punch before joining his friend in the dirt. One of the young men ran as soon as he had seen Terrence lunge from the shadows. The other two stood their ground and slammed their fists into Terrence's chest.

Terrence still managed to throw a few punches their way; his fist was weighed down by the knife in his hand. These kids were tougher than he had originally thought they would be. Survival, Terrence decided, was a strong motivation. He pictured these two with their feet against Leonard's head, and another burst of anger raged through his body.

Terrence's fist collided with a face and sent the teen hurtling to the ground. As he turned to take on the final kid, he heard the familiar sound of an opening switchblade. Fear flashed over him briefly, but was soon relegated to the back of his mind. He stared the kid in his eyes and flipped his own blade open.

"What the fuck are you doing, man?" The teen was out of breath and scared. He thrust his knife forward, but Terrence easily dodged it.

Hatred burned in Terrence's pupils. He knew he was face to face with the one who had hurt Leonard, and he wanted revenge. He felt the old instincts returning to him, yet he could not suppress them. Did he even want to?

The teen jumped forward in a clumsy attack. Terrence slapped the knife out of his hand and pinned him to the ground. His knee dug into the boy's throat as he coughed and gasped. Terrence felt a sadistic urge welling inside him.

"You like hurting old men?" Spit flew from his tongue into the boy's face. "You like kicking and beating old men until you kill them? Is that right?"

Unable to talk, and barely able to breathe, the young man tried to shake his head. His arms flailed wildly; his fists punched Terrence's side though they could not muster enough force to dislodge him. Terrence lifted his weight off of the boy just enough to allow him to speak.

"Answer me, God dammit!" He yelled into the kid's face.

"I...I'm sorry." His voice was raspy and soft. He choked up the words and coughed them out of his mouth. His face suddenly flooded with tears; he repeated his apology over and over.

Terrence's breath caught as he stared at the terrified boy's face. The knife in his hand trembled, and he felt his entire body go limp. What the hell was he doing? Was he going to kill this kid in cold blood? Was that the man he was now? Hadn't he changed at all through his time in prison, on the run, or with his wife? Terrence felt sick to his stomach. He lifted himself off the teenager and plopped into the dirt.

The young man jumped to his feet and tore off into the night. His friends had long since abandoned him, and were probably getting in contact with the police or their friends. Terrence knew he would have to hurry away before they returned with more people, and weapons.

He forced himself off the ground and to his car. As he reached for the handle, he noticed the knife still clutched in his hand. He coughed back a sob and hurled it into the park. Terrence got into his car and sped away. It would be another long night for him, indeed.

Chapter 44

"Get the fuck up!" the voice was brutal and terrifying. Larry's arm was jerked so hard that he thought it might have been pulled from the socket. The back of his head ached; blood dampened his eyes as it rushed from a cut in his forehead. He was dazed and nauseous. With only a hint of awareness, Larry felt himself being dragged through the front door of the MegaSaver.

"Up the stairs!" Larry grabbed the railing to steady himself as he was pushed up the staircase. He barely made each step; he was scared that he would fall backwards at any moment and that the gun pressing tightly against his back would accidentally go off. He was almost grateful to be shoved to the floor of his office once they made it in.

"Open up the goddamn safe!" Larry lay motionless on the floor for a split second. He contemplated his next move. Maybe he could jump the guy and take the gun away from him. Maybe he could push him aside and run out of the store without being shot. Maybe he should just give him the money and let him be on his way. Before he could come to a conclusion, he was grabbed by the neck and his head lifted up.

"Listen, motherfucker. I'm not fucking around with you." The voice was a razor dancing along the edge. "I said open up the goddamn safe." The sound of the trigger clicking back cemented Larry's decision. He would hand over the money.

"Okay, okay. It's right over here." Larry crawled over to the safe and began punching in the combination. Blood clouded his eyes, and his fingers bounced back and forth. The safe scolded him with a buzzing sound as he mistyped the numbers. He cursed and tried again.

"What the fuck are you doing, over there? Are you testing me?" Larry shivered as the man grew more and more agitated. He had been robbed only once before, but it was not like this. It had been a Mexican man; a big guy, covered in tattoos. He kept his nerves calm and his voice low. The gun he held was more for added effect than a weapon; the man himself was quite capable of killing someone with his bare hands. The Mexican had come and gone in under a minute, never having raised his voice above normal. This man was completely different.

"I'm trying, I'm trying." Larry took a deep breath and steadied his hand. He punched each button decidedly and with force. He exhaled as the distinctive "click" sounded from just inside the safe door. He pulled back on the lever, and the door swung open. Before he could do anything else, he was yanked backwards by the shoulder. He collapsed on the floor in pain and fear.

The robber stepped in front of the safe and grabbed the deposit bag. He ripped the zipper open and began flipping through the bills inside. Larry finally worked up the nerve to take a look at the man in front of him. His eyes darted around the man's physique to find any weakness he could use. The only two things he could focus on, however, was the magnum in his hand and the snake tattoo on his wrist.

"What the fuck is this?" The robber turned around and angrily flung the empty deposit bag at Larry. The man waved the meager stack of bills around. "Is this all the fucking money you made today?"

"Yes. That's all there is." Larry kept his eyes down at his feet; he thought it best not to look the man in the face. He cursed himself for ever staying this late with Maxine. If only he would have left sooner, he probably wouldn't be facing death at this moment.

"Listen, fucker." The man stepped forward and grabbed Larry's chin. He yanked up hard and stuck the barrel of his gun to the side of Larry's temple. His face moved in close, and his voice lowered. "I told you I'm not fucking around here. If you've got dough stashed anywhere else, you better fucking tell me now."

167

Larry's forehead instantly dampened with sweat, and a tight pain in his bladder began throbbing. Tears welled in his eyes, and he gently shook his head.

"There's about two hundred more in the change box, but it's all rolled coins." Larry cringed with each word.

"You've got to be fucking kidding me!" The man returned to the safe. He smashed the locked box onto Larry's desk with such a force that it exploded. Coins shot across the room in every direction as they burst from their paper rolls. The man stepped back towards Larry and lifted his gun.

"Fucking pathetic. I ought to kill you just for wasting my fucking time." The man shoved the gun back into Larry's face.

Larry's mind raced. There had to be something he could say, something he could do to get out of this. He'd negotiated high pressure deals with vendors. He'd hired and fired the best and worst of the bunch. He'd held off lawsuit after lawsuit of wrongful terminations. Surely, he could talk his way out of this.

"You fucking shit. A store like this should easily pull a few thousand." The man smirked. "I'd be doing your company a fucking favor by getting rid of you."

"Wait!" Before he knew what he was doing, Larry had yelled the words. "You've killed people before?"

"Yeah, fucker. I have. You're not fucking around with some kid who doesn't know what he's doing. I'm a fucking professional." The barrel dug into Larry's head with each word, causing a bruise to form.

"Good....good!" Larry stared the man directly in the eyes. Confusion swept across them and the gun barrel loosened slightly. "How would you like to walk away with $10,000?"

Chapter 45

Maxine's car glided into her parking space in the lot at her apartment. She opened the driver side door, gathered up her belongings, and hit the lock button on her side. She smiled to herself as she thought of how often she had had to lean across the seat to do that. Now, with Larry's help, she could not only lock the door the correct way, but her car always started and the knocking sounds had gone away.

Maxine made her way past the fighting couple's door and opened her own. She stepped in and flipped a switch; the room lit in a way that almost seemed magical. Once again, Larry had saved the day.

Tired and sore, Maxine made her way into the bathroom. She started the hot water in the bath tub and dropped in some bubble bath. She turned on her new boom box and pressed "play" on the CD player. Aretha Franklin's voice soared through the air of the apartment. On her way back to the bedroom, Maxine moved to the music; she sang along with joy and triumph.

She sat down on her bed and removed her shoes. She rubbed her hands up and down her feet massaging the pain away. Next, she removed her Capri pants. The skin on her knees was dark and dry; she grabbed a bottle of lotion and rubbed it in. A grunt of disgust slipped from her mouth as she thought of the reasons her knees looked bad.

Finally, Maxine stood and removed the last of her clothing. She stared at the curves of her body in her full length mirror. Her large breasts hung from her chest like overburdened tree limbs; love handles drooped from each side of her hips like wilted flowers. Maxine grabbed herself. She pulled slabs of loose skin up and tightened them; she mentally tried on her new self that Larry's money was going to pay for. A nip here, a tuck there; she would remake her body into a form more pleasing to her eyes.

Maxine's hands reached her stomach and paused. A wry smile formed on her lips, and she laughed to herself. As she stared at her figure, Maxine leaned back and stuck her stomach out. She exhaled and cradled her belly.

"Oh, Larry, this is your baby growing inside me." Maxine practiced in front of the mirror. "What should we name it? How about Aretha if it's a girl and Larry Jr. if it's a boy?"

Maxine rocked back and forth, holding her stomach.

"When little Larry or Aretha gets old enough, I'm sure he or she would love to play with your daughter. We can spend all day at the park and get them together for slumber parties when they're older."

Maxine laughed again as she pictured Larry's dumb-stricken face when she told him. It was all she could do to keep herself together when she saw him falling towards the floor. What an asshole.

She couldn't believe it had been that easy. She hadn't even heard herself say the words. One flicker in the back of her mind; a spark of imagination. It was out of her mouth before she realized it. Was that all it was really going to take?

Maxine stroked her flabby stomach once again and chuckled. She made her way back to the bathroom and climbed into the warm water. She leaned back, immersing herself in the bubbles. She dipped a rag and covered her face with it. She pictured Larry's horrified look one last time and smirked.

"White people…." She said to herself. "They'll believe any damn thing."

Chapter 46

The music at the Platinum Pony was louder than normal as naked women grinded in the laps of drunken businessmen and old perverts. A semi-attractive dancer writhed around the stage, scooping up dollar bills as a Def Leopard song blasted through the speakers. The air was artificially cold; stale cigarette smoke danced in the fake wind above the heads of patrons. Two-for-one specials kept the front seats by the stage filled, leaving an empty booth in the back of the club for Larry and Roland to sit in.

"This is where you wanted to talk?" Roland's eyes darted around looking for any sign of police or suspicious bouncers.

Larry downed his second shot of whiskey to ease the pang at the back of his head. His nerves had finally calmed down, and his heart had stopped racing. He felt more relaxed in a room full of people, assuming the man wouldn't kill him here.

"Look man, no one can hear us, and no one's paying any attention to a couple of guys sitting in the corner while they got snatch in their face." Larry's tone had begun to return to its condescending norm.

Roland eyed Larry suspiciously for a moment before finally accepting his logic. He took a sip of his drink and lit up a cigarette. His eyes kept a lock on the front door just in case.

"You told me you could get me $10,000." Roland's voice barely eased over the music.

"I need…a favor." Larry licked his lips and sipped his next shot.

"Yeah, you said that." Roland was becoming impatient. "What kind of favor?"

Larry moved his hand towards Roland's pack of cigarettes. His eyes asked permission. Roland's granted it. Larry lit and took a drag. He exhaled slowly.

"I need to….get rid of someone." Larry finally answered.

Roland's eyes squinted.

"Who?" Roland took a drag.

"One of my employees." Larry looked around to make sure he wasn't being heard. The only men even close to them were busy bouncing topless women up and down on their knees.

Roland leaned back. An employee….. His mind flashed to the man he saw leaving the store last night. The man that he had once shared a prison work detail with all those years ago. What did Larry know about that? Perhaps Terrence had been stealing money from Larry. Maybe he had slept with his wife. Maybe Larry had blackmailed him, and it was going sour. Roland realized he didn't care why Larry wanted him dead; he was only concerned with how much Larry knew about the man's past.

"Alright," Roland slowly nodded his head.

Larry quickly took a drag and exhaled. His stomach twitched for a second as adrenaline kicked in. He was both excited and nervous by the prospect of his proposal. He reached into his pocket and pulled out a folded sheet of paper. Looking around again to check their anonymity, Larry pushed the paper across the table towards Roland.

"Here's a picture." Larry tapped the paper twice.

Roland stuck the cigarette between his lips and slid his hand forward to grab the paper. He realized his heart rate had increased. He wasn't sure exactly what he was feeling; it was something between satisfaction and remorse. He'd once liked the kid, but jealousy had now corroded his emotion. If Roland couldn't have the life he wanted, then why should that little shit? Roland unfolded the paper. His eyes widened, and the cigarette nearly fell from his lips.

"What the fuck is this?" Roland stared at the picture of Maxine from her Employee of the Month award.

Larry's brow furrowed, and the pitch of his voice rose slightly. "That's the woman I need….to get rid of."

Roland's eyes darted back and forth from the photo to Larry's face. What the fuck was going on here? Why weren't these pieces fitting together?

"Why her?" was the only thing that came to Roland's lips.

Larry stabbed out his cigarette and downed the rest of his shot.

"Does it matter?"

Roland nodded without speaking.

Larry stared down at the shot glass and turned it around in his hand. "Because she's threatening to tell my wife about the affair we've been having."

Roland stared silently at the photograph for a second. Without warning, laughter erupted from his lips.

"What the fuck, man? Her?" Roland laughed loudly and stared at Larry.

"Yes, her." Larry's feathers were beginning to ruffle.

"You can't just fire the bitch or something?" Roland was truly amused by the situation.

"No, it's complicated." Larry was gruff and embarrassed. "She's pregnant."

Roland's laughter paused. "With your kid?"

"Yeah." Larry grunted the word.

Roland's laughter burst forth again, and he downed his shot.

"Listen, will you do it or not?" Larry's pride had kicked in.

The laughter died, and Roland's face took on its serious demeanor again. He took a drag from his Marlboro and looked into Larry's eyes.

"Alright. I kill this bitch, and you give me $10,000."

"That's right." Larry's voice had lowered.

"You must do alright for a fucking grocery store manager to have that much dough lying around."

"Fuck, I don't have that kind of money." Larry scorned. Roland's teeth clenched. "But, the store does. Next Thursday night, the money's gonna be in the safe in my office. I'll make sure to have Maxine there for some reason. All you have to do is make it look like a robbery gone bad."

"A robbery gone bad?" Roland took another drag.

"Yeah. I'll have all the cameras and shit off, so they won't see what happened. You walk in, shoot her, and I'll give you the money. I'll call 911 and tell them two black guys came in and did it or something." Larry practically boasted his plan.

"I see." The wheels began turning in Roland's mind.

"You win, I win. Get it? After the deal, you ride off to Mexico or somewhere, and I go home to my wife and kid." Larry took out his wallet and dropped a twenty dollar bill onto the table. "Everything works out."

Roland's hand flew towards Larry's palm. Before Larry could even react, his hand was empty. Roland pulled the wallet towards himself and opened it.

He removed Larry's driver license from the wallet. "Alright, Larry. I'm gonna hang on to this until Thursday night. That way, in case some pig comes bursting into my hotel room or happens to be waiting behind the store that night, I know where to find you."

Roland flipped Larry's wallet back to him. Larry's eyes moistened, and he stammered.

"Don't worry. It's not a trick!" Larry shoved his wallet back into his pocket.

"It better not be." Roland stared at Larry. "I promise you don't want to fuck with me."

Larry nodded his head and stood up. Without another word, he rushed out of the club.

A perky waitress came up to Roland's table with a drink tray in her hand.

"You want another shot, honey?" her fake smile and see-through shirt begged for tip money.

"I think I will." The waitress walked off to get the drink. Roland picked up his lighter and lit the edge of Maxine's picture. The fire quickly engulfed the paper as he dropped it into the ashtray. Within seconds, the waitress had reappeared with Roland's drink, and Maxine's photo had become a small pile of ash.

Chapter 47

The sun was bright and scorched the air around the MegaSaver. Shoppers stumbled through the parking lot, blinded by the light and drained from the heat. Their damp bodies clung to their clothing as if desperate for contact. With their eyes squinted and their foreheads soaked, everyone looked absolutely miserable as they entered the front door. Everyone that is, except for Larry Prescott.

Despite the fact that he had stayed out until the wee hours of the morning, had been beaten and thrown to the ground, and had the shock of his life, he looked vibrant and cheerful. He strolled through the front door of the MegaSaver, nodding to each customer he passed. His mouth was barely curled at each end, not so much a smile as a sneer. There was a slight bounce to each step and a glint of hope in each eye. The pain in the back of his head was only mildly uncomfortable; the road to happiness blocked only by one obstacle.

Maxine stood at the customer service desk with her back towards Larry. Though she didn't make a show of it, she was keenly aware of Larry's entrance. She fumbled around with her inconsequential paperwork, hoping to string out any awkwardness that was left over from the night before. She too had a smirk on her face that she couldn't quite hide.

"Good morning, Maxine." Larry's tone was a little too bright, and a bit formal. Her eyes flashed a wide look of surprise as she turned towards Larry's bruised and slightly swollen face.

"What the hell happened to you?" Unrehearsed shock rang from each word she spoke.

"What are you talking about?" He had briefly forgotten the battered figure that had greeted him from the mirror just an hour ago. He lifted a hand to his face and the dull pain his touch brought instantly reminded him. "Oh, I had a few too many last night, and missed the first step on the porch."

Maxine stared at Larry's face in disbelief. She knew him too well to believe anything that came from his mouth these days, though she couldn't really come up with a more plausible story.

"Really?" she cocked her head as she read his face for any hint of dishonesty.

"Yeah," Larry continued in his cheerful manner, "the wife had to help me up to the bathroom. I spent most of the night over the toilet."

Maxine's eyes became slits in her face. She knew he was lying, but had no way to prove it. She had come in this morning with the upper hand, or so she thought, and was determined to keep it. She drew the first card from her sleeve.

"Oh, I feel you," she rubbed her stomach with her hand, "I was up all morning doing the same thing."

"Wow, that's too bad." Larry could no longer force back his smile. "You should probably go to the doctor and get that checked out."

As Larry turned triumphantly towards his office, Maxine closed her open mouth. She'd played her best hand, and somehow he had an ace in the hole. Something was going on with him, and she didn't like it. Maxine thought for a moment. Should she give up and take the pitiful amount of money he offered her? He was hiding something, and she wasn't sure she could bully him into more. On the other hand, if she could turn up the heat and sufficiently unnerve him, he may cave. She decided that she had little to lose, and placed her bets on the table.

Larry was half-way up the stairs to his office when Maxine caught up with him. He kept his course, and never turned to face her as she spoke.

"You know, I was thinking it might be a good idea if I did go to the doctor." Her voice carried through the stairwell and into the hallway. "I've been sick every morning this week."

"Sounds like it could be something serious." Larry entered his office and sat down at his desk. His gaze focused on the paperwork in front of him; the smirk never faded from his face.

"I hope not." Maxine's tone took on a hint of desperation. "I've been feeling a little weak lately, too."

"Maybe it's a vitamin deficiency. " He shuffled his forms.

"I guess it could be," She would not yield. "I should probably get a test or something run. Maybe an X-ray or even an ultrasound."

Larry finally looked up towards Maxine.

"You know," she continued, "just in case it's kidney stones or something."

Larry and Maxine's eyes locked; each determined to take control of the situation. The air between them became thick with hostility. Neither of them spoke, perhaps afraid that a word could initiate a bloody duel.

"Am I interrupting anything?" Terrence finally broke the weighty silence in the room.

"No, Maxine was just leaving." Larry formally declared himself the victor.

"That's right," Maxine would not throw in the towel, "Larry just gave me the rest of the day off to go to the doctor."

"Oh?" Terrence's eyes danced between the two.

"Yeah," Maxine's hand cradled her stomach once more, "I've been having some stomach problems the past couple of days."

Larry sighed as she left the room. She had been a worthy adversary, and with her parting words had announced her plans for a rematch. Terrence watched the awkward exchange with tired eyes.

"Did you need something?" Larry's tone took on its usual gruffness.

"I was just going to ask if you know when the security guard was supposed to be here." Terrence let the information sink in.

"What security guard?" Larry's words were outlined with worry.

"The one Standland brought in. He said he talked to you about it." Terrence let his words slice Larry's pride.

"No, he didn't." Larry's eyes lowered as he tried to think. Had Standland told him?

Larry looked up and realized that Terrence was still in the office.

"Fine. Thank you." Terrence huffed and exited the office.

Fuck. The pain in the back of his head began to pound again. Larry rubbed his temples with his hands and tried to clear his thoughts. Should he go through with this now? What was the alternative? He couldn't have some little mixed Larry Jr. running around fucking up his life and marriage. Maybe he could still reason with Maxine. Maybe he could offer her the $10, 000 to get rid of the pregnancy.

Seeing yet another light at the end of the tunnel, Larry relaxed once more. Leaning back in his chair, he combed through paperwork. A brown envelope caught his attention. There was no address, no labels, and nothing to identify who it was from. There was only his name, written in big black marker.

Larry opened the envelope with a slight rumbling in his stomach. His hands began shaking, and sweat permeated his forehead as he looked through the contents. The pain in his head now raged, and he felt as if he may vomit. There was no question now of what he had to do. He had to get Roland his money.

Larry pulled the stalwart bottle from his drawer and took an early morning swig to calm his nerves. He took the envelope and its contents over to his paper shredder. With a flip of the switch, the machine whirred like a buzz saw. Larry fed the paper into the machine, watching it being ripped to shreds as he sipped his whiskey. When it was finished, her turned the machine off and replaced the bottle in his drawer. He walked towards the door and turned off his office light. He decided he would also take the rest of the day off, too. As he came up with some excuse to give Terrence, Larry thought about the Polaroids of his daughter that he had just destroyed and a chill ran down his spine.

Chapter 48

Terrence stood by the produce table, sorting through tomatoes. The firm ones, he placed back; the softer ones he placed to the side. He rolled the tomatoes around in his hand, like a baseball. He was finding a large amount of bad ones, meaning the produce manager had not been doing his job. Usually, Terrence would be having an angry discussion with the employee about it. Today, however, his mind was elsewhere.

Images from the night before kept creeping into his head. He could feel the kids' flesh in his hands. He could hear their yells and see their bloodied faces lying in the dirt. He kept an eye over his shoulder all morning, waiting for the police to walk in at any moment. His hands had already been fluttering when he walked into whatever the hell was going on in Larry's office.

It had only been a few days ago that Terrence had learned of the affair between Maxine and Larry. He wondered how the hell it had started. How long had it been going on? Terrence had always thought Maxine drove Larry crazy. The two men had spent a large amount of time in meetings trying to figure out what to do with her. She was a fairly competent worker, even if she thwarted Larry's authority. On more than one occasion, he had talked Larry out of firing her. And now they were fucking. It just didn't make sense.

Terrence had an uneasy feeling in his stomach. Something about this situation was not right. Money had disappeared from the deposit; Larry was frequently missing work. The situation had all the makings for a disaster. If Michael Standland caught wind of either the affair or the shortage, he was likely to get the police involved. That was the last thing Terrence wanted. He had made a small, quiet life for himself in the past few years, and he was determined not to lose it over some bullshit like this. Why did everything have to be so fucked up right now?

He rolled another tomato around in his hand. Its skin buckled under the slight pressure; a warm goo oozed onto his fingers. Terrence looked down to wipe his hand off as Maxine approached him.

"Well, I'm leaving now." Terrence raised his head to face Maxine. Her name badge was off, and she was carrying the large purse she had recently bought at the local flea market.

"Alright, I hope you feel better soon." He kept the suspicion from his voice.

"Me too, darling." The sugary sweetness coated Maxine's words. "I swear it feels like something is kicking around inside there!"

Maxine snickered as she walked away.

Terrence furrowed his brow. There's no fucking way she's pregnant. He couldn't remember the last time he had looked through her personnel file, but he was sure Maxine had to be in her late forties. Surely, that's not what she was talking about.

After a moment, Terrence watched Larry stomp down his office stairs. Larry looked around briefly before zeroing in on Terrence and heading his way. He noticed that his boss looked much more disconcerted than he had just a few minutes ago. This might normally raise flags in Terrence's mind, but Larry's emotions had become especially erratic lately.

"I have to leave for the rest of the day." Terrence could smell whiskey on Larry's breath. Damn, he starts early.

"Everything alright?" Terrence couldn't help but tighten the screw a little. He hoped something would drop out.

"Yeah, my kid's sick or something, and I gotta go take care of her." Larry was already turning as he spoke. He obviously hadn't cared if Terrence believed him or not.

Terrence tossed another tomato to the side and wiped his hands again. He wished that he could follow both of them to find out what was going on. Unfortunately, he was the only one left in charge and couldn't.

As Larry exited the store, he almost bumped into Michael Standland, who was entering. Terrence watched as the two spoke briefly. Larry kept going, and Standland shook his head; he then headed over to Terrence.

"Terrence, how are you?" Standland stated rather than questioned. "Where's Larry going?"

"He said his kid was sick."

Standland looked down to collect his thoughts.

"And where is Maxine?" His eyes squinted slightly.

"She said she was going to the doctor. Something about her stomach." He could feel Standland's concern growing.

"Hmmm....does this kind of thing happen often?" Standland seemed very troubled.

"Well...." Terrence began.

"Because, what I'm concerned about..." Standland interrupted "is the lack of coverage in the store now. This giveaway is only a couple of days away, and I'm not feeling very confident right now."

Terrence nodded his head. He understood more than Standland could have.

"Terrence, let's go have a chat in the office real quick." Standland clapped him around the shoulder and led him towards the stairs.

Chapter 49

Stanley Watson walked around the MegaSaver, staring more at the shelves of food than at the people he was supposed to be watching. His uniform clung tightly to his large frame; with each step the keys and gun jingled from his belt. His mouth hung slightly open as the only real means of getting oxygen into his body. His breath was loud and forced; even in the air conditioned store, he began to sweat.

He had worked as a security guard for the past ten years. During that time, he had watched over warehouses, clothing stores, banks, and the occasional party. But, his favorite had always been the grocery stores. There was rarely any shoplifting, and he was surrounded by all the food he could imagine. He normally sat by the exit door and said goodbye to customers as they left. When he was bored, he had the perfect excuse to walk around. When he was hungry, he was in heaven.

Stanley turned the corner of the aisle and nodded to a woman sifting through bags of chicken tenders. She was loudly bragging about hooking up with her "baby daddy's" best friend to someone over the phone. She paid no attention to the children surrounding her as she went into graphic detail about the size of his penis and the positions he put her in. She laughed loudly as she explained she could barely walk. Stanley briefly thought about asking her to quiet down, but his attention turned elsewhere. There, standing straight in front of him, like a beacon in a heavy fog, was a display of half price snack cakes.

Stanley stared at the display for several seconds without moving. The vast array of colorful boxes before him had him hypnotized; it took him a few moments to wipe the saliva from his mouth. His eyes danced around the shelf, taking in the junk food in all its glory. Which one should he get? There were a number of options. Some, he had loved as a child; he remembered how his mother packed them away in his lunch box. Others, he had recently grown to love; he would often stop by the convenience store on his way home from a late night shift to pick up a box or two. He finally narrowed his options to the yellow cream filled cakes and the chocolate squares with jelly inside. He decided to indulge himself and grabbed a box of each from the shelf.

Stanley quickly made his way to the front registers. He stopped by the drink cooler and grabbed two cans of soda to wash the delicious cakes down with. He took his items to register five where the chubby cashier smiled broadly at him.

"Oooh, these are SO good!" she beamed at Stanley's decision.

Stanley nodded his head, more interested in the food than the woman. He could practically feel the white cream cake slithering down his throat. The chubby cashier winced at him as she saw a string of spit dribble from his mouth. She quickly made his change and thrust it in his hand.

Stanley took his treasures back to the front door where he had placed a stool to rest on. He had already ripped one of the boxes open and was fumbling with the wrapper as he took his seat. He tore the plastic from the cakes and shoved a whole one in his mouth. The explosion of flavor was better than he had imagined. He cracked the can of soda open and drained it quickly. He was just about to devour the second cake when he was approached by Standland and Terrence.

"Hello, Stanley." Standland took his hand from Terrence's shoulder and extended it to the security guard.

Stanley shook the hand weakly and said hello.

"Terrence, this is your new security guard, Stanley." Standland smiled as he made the introduction. Stanley nodded his head towards Terrence, hoping to return to his desserts as soon as possible.

"Nice to meet you, Stanley." Terrence nodded in return.

As the two men resumed their course towards the stairs, Stanley tore into his next snack. Again, he washed it down with a can of soda. As he wiped sugary leftovers from his mouth, he leaned back on his stool and contemplated his new post. He would be very happy here, indeed.

Brad opened the door to his house and took a timid step inside. His foot crunched something that was probably a broken lamp. His next step kicked a piece of the end table that the lamp used to sit on. He made his way to the couch, surrounded by darkness. He couldn't bring himself to face the destruction he had caused the night before. He didn't need to see the broken pieces to know they were there.

Brad briefly considered smoking, but remembered he'd thrown everything out a few nights before. He couldn't crack open a beer or liquor bottle either, because he'd either drank or smashed them all 15 hours ago. The thought of food did not interest him in the slightest.

He sat alone in the darkness and thought. He was sick of everything. He couldn't stand working at the MegaSaver any more. At best, it was a shithole job that was going nowhere. He was tired of the pills and the powders. They had destroyed his life. They had driven his wife away and destroyed the house they had shared. And yet, they would not let him go. Their cold, tight grip remained around his throat; they dared him to defy them. They punished when he did.

A tear ran down Brad's cheek, and then another. A stream of sorrow ran from each eye and into the darkened room. Brad's body heaved with each sob. He buried his face into the couch cushion and yelled. His voice was full of rage; his throat a cannon of desperation. He was sick of feeling this way. In fact, he was sick of feeling anything at all.

When he could scream no longer, Brad sat up and wiped his eyes. He was vaguely aware of the aches that ran throughout his body. He lifted himself off the couch and shuffled to the bedroom.

He hadn't stepped foot in the room since his wife had left. He had slept on the couch most nights, if at all. Even during his mad cleaning rush, he had dealt with this room by closing the door. He paused for an instant before taking a step inside.

He bent down and picked up one of her shirts from the floor. He held it against his face and inhaled. Her scent was everywhere. He could smell the hairspray she used, the perfume she dabbed. The sheets were still ruffled from her last night in the bed. The blanket formed the curve of her body.

He threw the shirt across his shoulder and walked towards the closet door. He slid the accordion doors apart and peered inside. His pupils were briefly overcome by the light when he pulled the string, but they soon adjusted. They raced across each item on the shelf before finally settling on the back corner. Brad reached his hand towards the stack of old folded sweaters and slid under them. It took him a second, but he finally felt it. He pulled his hand back; the weight of the revolver was greater than he remembered.

There was a sliver of rust on the barrel. Brad couldn't remember the last time he had cleaned the gun, much less fired it. He flicked the chamber open and looked at the bullets that were already loaded. Brad took a deep breath and exhaled.

A million thoughts rushed through his mind as he stood there. Was he really going to do this? After everything that he had been through, was this really the answer? Would it really fix anything? Brad took another deep breath. He held it as the thoughts finally quieted. There was no going back. There was no second guessing. He knew what he had to do, and was prepared for it.

With a tug of the chord, Brad extinguished the closet light and walked back to the living room. The revolver was still firmly gripped in his hand.

Chapter 51

The sun blazed down onto a full parking lot at the MegaSaver. A constant stream of customers passed in and out of the doors hoping that they would have the magical receipt number for the $10,000 giveaway tomorrow.

Inside the store, it was near chaos. The lines at each register were backed up into the aisles. Stockers were hurriedly trying to fill shelves and tables, but were having little success. There were phone calls and customer complaints; returns and exchanges. Terrence ran from one end of the store to the other, attempting to keep the situation from boiling over.

Brad spent most of his time near the freezers and coolers. He was pale and sweaty. He remained quiet and brooding, and was having trouble concentrating on his duties. He made no eye contact with the other employees and avoided customers as much as possible.

Michael Standland was preoccupied with the decorations that were being displayed around the building. He was taking complete charge of the contest. He had people hanging signs throughout the store; he had them giving away flyers on the street. He even had a small stage built in front of the registers for the actual presentation.

Larry Prescott was even doing his share. He had spent most of the day at the customer service desk answering the phones and filling in for Maxine. She had been spending her time going back and forth between the registers and the bathroom. Each time she would return with a sick expression and a knowing glance towards Larry. In reality, she spent the time smoking a cigarette or filing her nails.

The employees kept busy and rarely made eye contact. Their talk was shallow and light; no one wanted to have an extended conversation. They each knew what they had to do that night, and focused on keeping their plans from everyone else.

Towards the late afternoon, Larry had retreated to his office. The rush of business and his plans for later were playing havoc with his nerves. He decided to enjoy the quiet of his private space, along with the comfort of a strong drink.

As he sipped his whiskey, he looked out over the store he had steered for the past few years. Everything about him was wrapped up in it. All of his money came from the store. Almost all of his time was spent at the store. Hell, for the past few weeks, even his most intimate moments occurred at the store. Although he felt things were as prepared for as could be, he could still feel it all slipping through his fingers.

Was he really going to be responsible for Maxine's death? He shuddered at the thought of it. The blood, the terror, the aftermath. Was he strong enough to make it through all of that? Would he crack under police interrogation? Would an autopsy reveal her pregnancy, and could they use DNA to determine that he was the father? Oh God. He had never thought of that until just this moment.

A pain shot through Larry's chest as his muscles clenched. What the fuck was he doing? If he had her killed, they were sure to find out that he was involved. What was the likelihood that the store would be robbed of prize money the day before it was to be given away, leaving Maxine the only one dead? Larry took a large swig from his bottle and rubbed his forehead. This was all going wrong. He didn't have the stomach for the deed at all.

But what could he do? Having a child with Maxine would ruin his life just as much as killing her would. His wife would surely leave him; he would most certainly be fired. Everything that he had worked for would crumble at his feet. Tears welled in his eyes as he began thinking of the other way out. He took another swig and wondered how painful it would be. How would he do it? A gun? A noose? Pills? Who would find him? What if Standland was the one? The thought repulsed him. No, he had spent too much time and energy in the world just to give up like that. There had to be another way. Almost on cue, Maxine knocked on the office door.

190

Larry looked up, tears still hovering in his pupils. He wiped them away quickly and tossed the bottle back in his desk drawer.

"Yeah, what is it?" There was no irritation in his voice; only resignation wrapped in defeat.

Maxine lowered her eyes to allow him a shred of dignity as he got himself together. Without even looking at him, she could tell that this was the moment she had been waiting for. She knew she could get him to break.

"Listen, Larry," Maxine's voice was soft and gentle. Her siren call lured him from his sinking boat. "I talked to the doctor the other day and…"

"Yeah, what is it?" Larry's voice was flat and despondent.

"Well, he thinks that it may not be a good idea for me to carry this baby to term." Maxine cast her line into the water.

"Really?" Larry's eyes lit up, and his head whipped to face her.

"Well, now I don't know that I agree with him on that." Maxine tugged to stir the lure.

"He is your doctor, Maxie. You should listen to him." Larry swam towards the hook.

"If I listened to every white man who knew what was good for me…" she caught her reaction before it could do permanent damage. "I'm sorry, my hormones are going wild."

"I understand," Larry nodded, still hopeful.

"Look, all I'm saying is that I could perhaps be persuaded to listen to him." Maxine felt a slight tug.

"Really? How?" Larry's future brightened, and he lunged for the hook.

Without speaking, Maxine shifted her eyes towards the safe. Larry understood immediately.

"Alright, how much?" Larry was instantly in business mode.

Maxine stared at him without saying a word.

"You want the prize money?" Larry took a stab.

The

"That's right, darling." Maxine began slowly pulling the lure towards the surface.

For a moment, neither spoke. Maxine let the demand hang in the air; she knew it was the answer to all of his problems and was sure he would take it. Meanwhile, Larry contemplated the logistics. How could he take the money, give it to her, avoid Roland, and do it all without going to jail? Maxine cleared her throat loudly, bringing Larry back into the moment.

"Alright," Larry clasped down in full force. "Meet me at the front door thirty minutes after closing. The security guard will be driving around the building, patrolling the lot. When he gets to the back of the store, come up to the front door, and I'll let you in."

"I'll be here." Maxine dumped Larry into the boat. A broad smile shone across her face. It was really going to happen.

As Maxine left the office, Larry took a deep breath. He wasn't out of the thick of it yet, but could see the light. There were just a few loose ends to tie up, and he would be free. He pulled the bottle from the drawer and took another swig. He then grabbed the phone and dialed his home number.

"Hey honey, it's me," he said when his wife answered. "I need you and the kid to spend the next few days at your mother's for me. I'll have to explain later."

Chapter 52

The sky was a mixture of reds, yellows, and blues at ten minutes to eight at the MegaSaver. The last few customers were strolling out of the store, and the parking lot was emptying. The day had been a long, busy one, and all of the employees were wiped out. The stockers rushed around, cleaning and filling shelves. They mopped floors, wiped the counters down, and washed the windows; Standland had made it clear that he wanted the store to be in perfect condition when the prize was given away in the morning. News crews from local television stations would be arriving just a few minutes after the store opened at 8:00 AM to broadcast the give-away thirty minutes later.

Larry had stayed in his office for the past couple of hours, while Maxine and Terrence had just left. Brad, meanwhile, paced anxiously in the bathroom. He had gone over and over his plan for the past few days, trying to psych himself up. He pictured fields of roses, clear swimming pools and imagined his wife's arms around him. Over and over again, he told himself it would be ok. His body argued vehemently. His stomach twisted into knots, his hands quaked, and his skin was clammy. Even his knee had been giving him trouble again.

Brad's plan was simple. He would hide in the cooler while the security guard made his final rounds throughout the store. He knew that Larry was keeping late hours at the store lately, and he hoped tonight would be no exception. Dressed in black, with a ski mask and his gun, Brad would force Larry to open the safe. He'd take the money and run to the rental car he had parked nearby. After everything blew over, Brad would surprise his wife with a vacation. He had even planned on renewing his vows at the clinic. Perhaps the receptionist, Denise, could preside over the ceremony.

Brad had played every detail through his mind a hundred times. He had watched all the managers for any sign of suspicion. He felt terrible about threatening Larry, but it was the only way. Now, as the day was coming to an end, and his plans were coming to a head, he found himself panicked and anxiety-ridden. He had even paid a visit to an old friend on his way in that morning.

He removed another pill from his pocket. He had already taken four of them during the day, hoping to calm his nerves. They had diminished the stress, but hadn't completely gotten rid of it. He swayed to the side, but caught himself. He paid no attention to the intoxication; he knew adrenaline and the second set of pills in his other pocket would focus him for the task at hand.

Suddenly, Brad heard footsteps. He jumped into a stall and climbed onto the toilet. The door creaked open; he listened as the man's lumbered breath echoed. Heavy steps fell onto the tile and moved into the connecting stall. Brad held his breath as he tried to remain calm. He looked down at the feet next to him. Dark brown pants fell to their ankles; a gun was attached to the belt. Fuck. It had to be the security guard. What if he checked this stall? Brad popped another pill to keep calm. How many was that now?

Strange sounds from the guard's stall stirred Brad to consciousness. Shit. Had he nodded off, again? He had to get out of there. He waited for another round of noises and crept down from the toilet. He tiptoed to the door and slowly opened it. The room had begun to spin by this point, and it was getting harder for Brad to keep his legs moving.

What was he supposed to do? A wave of nausea cramped his stomach, and he doubled over in pain. He heard water running somewhere, and he forced himself up. Without understanding exactly why, he knew he had to hide again. He stumbled towards a large medal door and pulled it open. The sting of frigid air burrowed through his aestheticized skin. Once inside, he pulled the door closed and took a seat on a box of frozen fries.

Through the haze of narcotics, Brad felt his body tingle. The sweat that had moistened his skin was now hardening. He became aware that his breath was not only visible, but that it was slowing as well. Something in the back of his brain was telling him that all was not right. Unfortunately, Brad could not force the pieces together enough to form a complete picture. Instead, he curled his body into a ball in the corner. The rumble of the compressor fans lulled him towards sleep.

Clutching his blue tinted skin, Brad closed his eyes and pictured his wife. He imagined the first time they met, the first time they made love. He thought about the day he had proposed to her and the day they went to the courthouse to get the paperwork signed. He thought of all the time they had shared on their couch in front of the television; the bowls they smoked must have numbered in the hundreds. He remembered the day she walked out on him and the ultimatum she had given. He smiled slightly as he envisioned the resort where they would soon rekindle their love, and all the time that lay before them.

Clouds of vapor puffed from his lips as he lay on the floor of the freezer whispering his wife's name. As he closed his eyes for the last time, the frozen air stripped his body of life. His breath faded, and his heart slowed to stillness. There, amongst the pallets of chicken wings and Vietnamese catfish, Brad faded away. He would never realize that he had picked the wrong door.

Chapter 53

As the final customer made her way out of the store, Larry paced nervously by the front door. There was a sick feeling in the pit of his stomach, and his eyes perused the parking lot just beyond the glass. Somewhere out there, he knew there was a vicious killer waiting. Larry hoped that there was enough time to get the money, give it to Maxine, and get her out before Roland showed up. Once she was gone, he would wait for Roland with his .38 in hand. All Larry had to do was get him to turn his back, and everything would be taken care of. He would then blame the robbery on a second man who had escaped.

Larry turned the key on the front door of the MegaSaver and climbed the stairs to his office. He studied the parking lot from his window; he saw no sign of danger outside. There was only the security guard, Stanley, walking around, smoking and eating a pie.

Larry turned and stared at the safe. Earlier in the day, he had watched as the armored car service delivered the money. How much fucking trouble it was causing him. Just a couple of weeks ago, he would never have thought his life would take this direction. Things could change so quickly.

Larry walked to the security system that sat in the corner of his office. It was about 20 years old, and several of the cameras had stopped working. The black and white recorder could barely capture anything that happened out on the darkened parking lot. The low light on the inside fared little better. With a touch of a button, the obsolete VCR's gears stopped turning. No one would ever witness the events of that evening.

Larry turned the light off in his office and descended the stairs. As he exited the store, he said goodnight to the security guard. Stanley returned his salutation with his usual head nod; his mouth being too full to articulate words. Larry walked to his car and felt a buzz from his phone in his pocket. He removed the phone and read the text message Maxine had sent him. She was waiting for him around the corner of the building in her appointed spot. He snapped his fingers for show and turned back towards the MegaSaver.

"Hey, I forgot to grab some reports off my desk. I gotta run back in and get them." Larry had stopped at Stanley's car.

"You need me to go in with you?" Stanley had just opened another soda to wash his snack down with.

"No, no. It's okay. Go ahead and start making your rounds. I'll only be a minute." Larry tried to force his voice into as nonchalant a tone as possible.

Without a word, Stanley chugged his soda and tapped the accelerator on his car. The yellow lights at the top flashed across the dark parking lot. Larry turned back to the store and opened the door. He stood motionless for a second, watching the lights disappear around the side of the building. A dark figure approached him from the opposite side. His heart pounded for a few beats as the shadow drew near. He sighed in relief to see Maxine.

"Hurry up!" Larry barked at Maxine. The two of them rushed into the building, and Larry locked the door.

Chapter 54

The night air was hot and humid; it fogged the windows of Terrence's car and clung to his skin with fervor. He sat in the darkness of an alleyway across the street from the MegaSaver. Though he had clocked out hours ago, he decided it would be in his best interest to stick around. He sat, watching the parking lot as customers came and went. As the night drew near, he became more and more apprehensive.

He couldn't exactly put his finger on it, but something felt terribly wrong. There were too many strange things going on around him; people's demeanors, their attitudes and mannerisms betrayed their light-hearted words. At first, he had been pleased when Standland told him a security guard would be hired. Terrence couldn't watch everyone all the time. Unfortunately, Standland's choice of guards left everything to be desired. Unless someone was stealing a bag of chips, Terrence doubted the guard would even notice.

Before he left that day, he had decided that if something was going to happen at the store, it would have to be that night. There would be too many people crawling all over the place in the morning. He knew Standland planned to arrive at six thirty for final touches and inspection. Larry would probably drag himself in around seven forty-five; the security guard would still be there that morning. Add in the news crews and crowds of customers, and it would make one hell of a circus. No, if something was going to happen, it would be tonight.

Terrence wiped perspiration from his forehead and rubbed his eyes. He checked his watch for the time: eight o'clock on the dot. He watched as the last customer walked her bags out to her car and drove off. He knew that Larry had been staying late over the past few days and wondered if tonight would be any different. Maxine had left before Terrence, so he doubted that she would be a factor. He kept his eyes focused on the front door.

The light in Larry's office blinked out a moment later; surprising Terrence. He watched as Larry exited the building and said goodnight to the guard. He couldn't believe that everything might be alright. Larry would almost surely be involved in anything that happened here tonight; Terrence decided that perhaps he had been worried for nothing. He kept his eyes on Larry's movements. He made it all the way up to his car and then stopped. Terrence's heart jumped as he saw Larry pull his phone out and head back towards the building.

As the security guard drove around to the back of the store, Terrence saw a figure move around the other side. His suspicions now confirmed, he had to plan his next move. He decided that the best plan of action would be to call Larry's phone and tell him he was being watched. If Larry knew someone was on to him, he would probably give up and go home. After all the hoopla died down, the three of them could discuss everything and work it out with no legal action.

Larry and Maxine entered the building and headed up the steps. Terrence watched as the light came on in Larry's office again. Now was the time to call. He pulled out his cell phone and began dialing Larry's number. As his finger moved to the "call" button, Terrence saw another figure move across the lot towards the MegaSaver. He lowered his phone and stared. He wasn't sure, but he thought he knew the figure.

The shadow darted across quickly and with resolve. He tugged on the door several times as if he expected it to open. The man grew angry and his movements more exaggerated. Terrence watched as the man turned to scan the parking lot for signs of security. The light illuminated the man's features, and Terrence's breath stopped.

It couldn't be. Terrence was frozen with shock as he watched the man pull a gun from his pants and shoot the lock on the door. It had been years since he had last seen Roland, but the man looked just as dangerous as before.

They had parted ways under bad terms the night after they had escaped the prison van. After making their way through fields and dirt roads, the two men had ended up in the city, combing the streets for food and a place to hide. They walked into the bus station just before dawn and sat themselves in the corner.

With no money, and rumbling stomachs, the men began watching the people around them. They had few options at that time in the morning; there were mostly vagrants and low-lifes like themselves with no other place to stay. Finally, a bus pulled up, and a few people got out. Roland's eyes had locked on to a woman wearing decent clothing and clutching a large purse.

With a tug of the arm, Roland summoned Terrence to the back of the station. They waited in the burgeoning morning light as the passengers found their cars or their rides. Terrence and Roland kept a lookout for the woman. She finally emerged from the station, coffee in hand. She dug through her purse, attempting to find her keys; Roland took that moment to strike.

As the woman rummaged, Roland snuck up behind her. His arm crashed into the back of her head, sending her to the pavement with a yelp. Hot coffee spewed into the woman's face, burning her eyes shut. She screamed in terror and begged him not to hurt her. Roland covered the woman's mouth and pitched the purse to Terrence. It hit the ground. Terrence stood completely still. He watched as the woman flailed on the pavement; her muffled shrieks brought a stream of vomit to his mouth. He was not the animal he once was, and could not bring himself to hurt the lady.

"What the fuck are you doing?" Roland snatched the purse and grabbed a wallet from it. As he pulled money and credit cards out, he tossed the wallet into the woman's face. She moaned with pain and tried to crawl away.

"Come on, man, let's leave." Terrence begged Roland to leave the woman alone.

Ignoring him, Roland raised a foot above the woman's head. "Shut the fuck up, bitch!"

Before Roland could bring his boot down across the back of the woman's head, Terrence tackled him to the ground. His fists flew down towards Roland's face, busting his lip and reopening his fresh wounds. The woman screamed and ran back towards the bus station.

Terrence turned to watch the woman run; Roland took the opportunity to crack Terrence's jaw. Terrence flew backwards in pain. He squirmed on the ground as Roland approached him, but before he could punch Terrence, a bus driver yelled towards the fighting men.

Roland spit on Terrence's face and took off running into the night. The bus driver ran up to Terrence and helped him to his feet. He led Terrence back into the station and sat him next to the woman he had just tried to rob. A worker from the cafeteria was cleaning the woman's scrapes and cuts; she handed Terrence an alcohol pad and gauze.

As Terrence cleaned his wounds, he waited for the police to come. He was already preparing himself for a return to prison when the woman turned to him.

"Thank you so much, young man." The woman dug through her purse. He stared blankly, trying to figure out what was going on. "That man would have killed me if you hadn't of run up to help me."

"Sure would have. He got you good, too!" The cafeteria worker admired Terrence's injuries.

Terrence opened his mouth to speak, but could not find the words. He was surprised and confused; this night had turned out nothing like he had planned.

"Here," the woman handed him two hundred dollar bills. "It's all I have on me."

Terrence stared at the money. "Oh, I can't…"

"No, I insist. I know it's not much, but it's the least I can do." The woman smiled at him. "You saved my life after all."

Terrence took the money and left the station. With it, he slowly got onto his feet and built the rest of his life. Although he had not kept track of Roland, he now realized that his former friend had not been so lucky. The years had worn on Roland, aging his skin and chilling his blood.

He watched as Roland flung the door to the MegaSaver open and stormed inside. The situation, whatever it was, had just become deadly, and Terrence knew that he had to do something. He jumped out of his car, grabbing the satchel from the front seat. He popped the trunk open and threw the bag inside. He slammed the door closed and made his way across the street. He only hoped that he could stop Roland before they all found the empty safe.

Final Chapter

Maxine rushed through the door of the MegaSaver. Larry hurriedly locked it and they both headed up the stairs. Maxine noticed that Larry moved quickly and kept looking back behind them.

"Come on. We only have a minute." He was chiding and breathing hard.

Larry and Maxine made their way to the office; he flipped the light switch as they entered. He glanced around the room and snuck a peek out of the window. Maxine's heart raced with excitement as she thought about the new life this money was about to bring her. Larry kneeled down to punch the combination into the safe; each beep of the button brought a tear to Maxine's eyes. It was all about to change for her. Her breath caught as she heard the door to the safe click and watched as Larry swung it open. Thank you God! Thank you so much for this little, bald, gold-covered cock!

"WHAT THE FUCK!?!?" Larry's voice echoed through the office. Maxine's heart stopped.

"What's wrong?" Maxine pushed Larry aside and stared at the safe. Her head spun, and her throat made a wincing noise. She steadied herself against Larry's desk.

"Where's the fucking money?" Maxine rarely used that word, but felt justified at the moment.

Larry flung his head towards Maxine. His eyes were red with fury; they became slits in his face, aimed to tear her's apart.

"Why don't you tell me?" His voice croaked in a way that terrified Maxine. She had never heard something more full of rage in her entire life.

"What do you mean, me?" she leaned over the desk, suddenly afraid that Larry might physically harm her.

"I saw that fucking money brought in here by the security service, myself!" Larry towered over Maxine. His skin

203

was on fire, and his teeth were clenched. "What the fuck did you do with it?"

"I…I…" Maxine tried for words, but they never came.

"What kind of a fucking scam are you trying to pull on me?" Larry's hands crept up as if they were making their way to Maxine's throat.

"It wasn't me! It wasn't me!" Tears streamed down her face as she raised her hands in defense.

"Are you even pregnant!" Larry didn't even bother with the question mark. In his heart, he knew the answer. He just needed to hear her say it.

Maxine shook her head, not knowing what the result would be.

Larry took a step towards Maxine. He wasn't sure what he would do; he was no longer in control of his actions. Here was the woman who had brought him to the verge of suicide with a lie. He was never in danger. There was no child. There was no threat. He had been willing to risk jail for the money that she had apparently already taken. He had been willing to risk his life by bringing a psychopathic hit man to the store… Oh shit. The hit man.

Larry suddenly jumped from Maxine over to the window. She shook her head and wiped tears away in amazement. Had he suddenly come to his senses? She watched Larry's body instantly switch from being tense with anger to shaking with fear. What the hell was going on?

Larry turned towards Maxine. His eyes were completely changed. They were wet with horror and glazed with panic. He rushed over to Maxine and grabbed her shoulders.

"Are you sure you didn't take the money?" Larry's voice was shrill.

"Why the hell would I come here tonight if I had?" Maxine's was the voice of reason.

Suddenly, there was a pounding downstairs on the door. Larry nearly flew out of his skin as he shoved Maxine out of the office door.

"We've got to get the hell out of here!" He was practically gliding down the stairs. Maxine was confused and disoriented, but decided to follow Larry's lead.

As they reached the bottom step, he turned sharply towards the back of the store. "Hurry! We have to go out the back way!"

The explosion behind them froze Maxine and Larry in their places. Maxine covered her face in fright. Larry turned to face the agent of vengeance he had unwittingly unleashed.

Roland stormed into the front door. His face was crimson with outrage; his mouth twitched. His eyes were ablaze, but focused. There was only one thing on his mind now, and he would take it by any means necessary.

Roland raised his magnum towards Maxine's face. He pulled the hammer back and smirked slightly.

"You must be Maxine." His words were quiet, but sharp.

Maxine nodded without speaking. She wondered how he knew her name.

"Larry's told me a lot about you." Roland's hand never wavered in its aim.

Maxine turned to face Larry. Her eyes questioned him silently; the look on his face was answer enough.

"He told me all about the time you've spent together," Roland took a step forward,"and all the trouble it's caused him."

Tears silently rolled down Maxine's cheek.

"You see, lover boy and I have an agreement," Roland nodded towards Larry. "Don't we lover boy?"

"Did he promise you the money upstairs?" Maxine cast a desperate line.

"You're a smart one." Roland smiled wryly. "I can see why he liked you."

Maxine's stance hardened from fear to defiance. If she was going to go down like this, she was taking Larry with her.

"Well, you're in for a disappointment," her words rang loud and true, "because it ain't up there."

Roland's eyes shot from Maxine's face to Larry's. Sweat poured from Larry's forehead, and he quickly stepped around Maxine. He raised his hands in fear and stammered.

"I swear, I didn't do it. I didn't know! There's only a couple of people who could have done it! We can still get it! It will have to be here in the morning! If you come back then…"

A sudden explosion silenced Larry's words, this time forever. The bullet ripped through the front of his skull and bore into the back of his head. Blood and brain matter were hurled through the air; they slammed into Maxine's face with such force that she stumbled backwards. Larry's lifeless body collapsed to the floor; blood streamed onto the recently shined tile.

For a moment, Maxine stared motionless. Her body was numb; her muscles became immoveable. Images of her childhood, her marriage, even her affair with Larry circled around her mind as her brain attempted to deal with what she had just seen. Slowly, as the enormity of the situation sank in, Maxine's mouth opened, and a scream tore from her lips.

Still unable to run, she raised her hands to wipe the pieces of gore from her face. Tears coursed from her eyes, and sobs bellowed from her chest. Roland smirked triumphantly and took a step toward her. He pulled the hammer back on his gun and raised it again.

"Now, Maxine. I want to know where the fucking money is before I blow the head off your fucking shoulders." Roland's voice was loud this time. He was starting to get pissed.

"She doesn't have it." Terrence's voice resonated from the front door of the MegaSaver.

Roland spun around to see Terrence's tall frame taking up the doorway.

"If it isn't my old friend," Roland hocked phlegm from his throat and spit it on the floor. "How ya been, kid?"

"Better than you, it looks like," Terrence looked Roland up and down. Life had taken its toll on the older man.

"Well, we can't all have nice houses in the suburbs, I guess." Roland's laugh was unnerving.

The concrete expression on Terrence's face fell. How did Roland know where he lived?

Maxine, finally able to move, slowly backed away. Her sneakers were barely able to avoid squeaking in the pool exuding from Larry's neck. She silently crept towards the back of the store.

"Not to mention the car, and the wife....Oh, the wife." Roland smiled.

Terrence took a step; Roland raised the gun to his chest.

"Now, she's a fine piece of ass. I must admit, even I was impressed. Where did you ever meet someone like her?"

"Church," Terrence's muscles flexed as he readied to pounce.

Roland's cackle serrated the air, as if he had just figured out the punch line to a bad joke. "That would explain all the praying…"

Terrence's stance loosened; his lips parted to form a question he didn't know if he could ask. Roland's eyes brightened, and his heels dug in.

"I couldn't stop myself from paying a visit to the little woman earlier today. I just got so curious as to how you could find someone like her."

Terrence's fingernails stabbed the palms of his hands.

"Naturally, we got to talking about the old days," Roland made direct eye contact with Terrence. "Imagine her surprise when she found out who she was married to. She didn't even know what your real fucking name was!"

Maxine rounded the corner of the freezer. She looked around, desperate to find somewhere to hide. She opened the door and snuck in. The cold air cut through her thin clothing, causing her to huddle down into a ball. She closed her eyes and prayed that she would make it out alive.

Terrence's teeth ground together as his breath was hurled from his nostrils. He would tear Roland apart with his bare hands.

"I really believe if she could have gotten those chords off her wrists, she would have attacked me." Roland added with intentional flippancy.

Terrance lunged for Roland. His hands hurled themselves towards Roland's face; an animal's roar seared through his open mouth. Roland squeezed the trigger and sent a bullet tearing through Terrence's flesh.

Maxine jumped at the sound of the gun shot. She swung around, as if to see through the metal wall of the freezer to watch what was happening at the front of the store. She slipped on a patch of ice, and fell forward. Her chin smacked the ground, knocking out one of her teeth. Blood gushed from her mouth, and she sobbed once again. She reached up to pull herself from the floor; her hand grasped something frozen and unnatural. Maxine yanked hard, pulling Brad's rigid corpse on top of her. She screamed uncontrollably, and kicked the body away from her.

She threw herself against the freezer door, and took off running towards the back of the store. Her feet barely touched the ground as she flew quickly towards the fire exit. A blast ripped behind her; suddenly she collapsed in agony. She took deep breaths and tried to look behind her. Blood was flowing from her left calf; she was unable to stand up, let alone run away.

Roland lowered his gun and began walking towards Maxine's writhing figure. His steps were slow and deliberate. He allowed the gravity of fear, and the pain of her wound to sink in for a moment. She had managed to turn over onto her back to face him by the time he got to her.

"Now, dear. I want to know what happened to the fucking money." Roland stared at Maxine as he loaded the chamber of his gun. "And I should warn you to tell the truth. The next bullet won't be as forgiving as the first." He kicked her leg, and Maxine winced in agony.

"So, where's my money?" Roland aimed the gun at Maxine's head.

"Fuck you, white boy." Maxine yanked an oversized can of yams from the shelf behind her. Her adrenaline in overdrive, she hurled the heavy tin towards Roland's crotch. It crushed him, instantly sending him to the ground.

Roland fell and clutched his precious organ. Fluid shot up his throat, and he choked up vomit. Another can came crashing down onto this head; Roland hit the floor and screamed in pain. He cradled his head in his hands. His fingers became moist with his own warm blood. His vision was filled with white spots, and dizziness threw him off balance.

Satisfied that Roland couldn't follow her, Maxine pulled herself up and tried to take a step towards the door. The pain in her leg was too great though, and she fell forward again. Roland howled in rage and anguish; Maxine looked around the store for anything that could help her escape. Her eyes fixed on the motorized handicap cart several feet in front of her. She scooted her way across the floor, leaving a trail of blood. Exhausted, she reached the cart and pulled herself into it. She flipped the switch and unplugged it from the charger; the cart pulled her forward at a snail's pace towards the back of the store.

Halfway towards freedom, a jar of mustard exploded on the shelf next to her. Several more items detonated around her as Roland raised his gun and fired. He pulled himself up, trying to steady his body against the shelf to sharpen his aim. The pain and nausea kept him from pulling the trigger again; he blindly stumbled after Maxine, hurling curses towards her like bombs.

Outside the store, Stanley was enjoying an unscheduled snack break in his car. Having pulled around the back, where he was sure Larry couldn't watch, Stanley feasted on the chips, cookies, and soda he had bought just before the store closed. The air conditioner cooled his stretched skin as his car idled in the back lot. The yellow lights flashed across the store's wall as they circled atop the car.

As he was stuffing the third cookie in his mouth, Stanley heard a noise coming from inside the store. He turned off the radio and rolled the window down. He took a bite and listened to yet another sound coming from inside. As he swallowed a chocolate chip, there was another pop. This time, he was sure he had heard it and was convinced it was gun fire.

Stanley rolled up his window and threw the car into gear. Dropping his bag of cookies in the passenger seat, he stabbed the gas pedal. The back tires squealed, sending smoke into the hot summer air. Just as the car lunged forward, the back door of the store flew open. Stanley was unable to stop the car from plowing directly into the woman on the handicap cart. There was a loud smash and a muffled scream as the figure was dragged underneath the security car. Stanley slammed his foot on the break and jumped out.

He rushed to the front of the car, where he saw Maxine lying with her eyes closed. She was unconscious, but still breathing. The cart lay crumpled underneath the car in a twisted pile of plastic and medal. Stanley panicked and let out a yelp. He turned back to the security car and flipped on the emergency radio. He yanked the microphone from its holder and opened his mouth to summon the police and an ambulance.

Two shots rang from the exit door and Stanley was thrown backwards. Roland emerged from the store; the barrel of his gun still smoking. He walked over to the security guard and fired another shot into his wide chest. Bleeding and sick, Roland limped over to Maxine's comatose body underneath the security car. He took the last of his rounds from his pocket and loaded them into his gun.

"You stupid fucking cunt." Roland hissed the words towards Maxine. "Do you realize all the fucking trouble you caused me? I just wanted the money! I just wanted to shoot you and your boyfriend in the face, take the money, and start a new life somewhere. But I guess you just couldn't understand something like that, could you? COULD YOU!?!?!"

Roland slammed the chamber back into the body of the gun. He pointed the barrel towards Maxine's head and pulled the hammer back.

"Now, I'm not gonna get anything, and you're still gonna die." Roland spit blood from his lips onto Maxine's face. "Doesn't seem very much fucking worth it, huh?"

"Not really."

Roland turned as five bullets erupted from the gun in Terrence's hand. They burst through rings of fire from the barrel and dug into Roland's chest. Roland flew backwards onto the ground, landing next to the lifeless security guard.

Terrence dropped Larry's gun and clutched his bleeding shoulder. He ripped the bottom part of his shirt and tied it around the wound. He slowly walked over to Maxine and checked her pulse. She was still alive, though barely. He turned towards Roland, surprised to find that he was still breathing. Roland's eyes focused on Terrence as he coughed blood from his ruptured torso.

With only moments left, Roland whispered to Terrence. "I guess you haven't changed as much as I thought, huh?"

Terrence clasped Roland on the shoulder and leaned in with words of his own.

"Sorry compadre. It's nothing personal."

A bitter laugh served as Roland's final comment. Clutching his wounded shoulder, Terrence headed into the store and dialed 911 from a phone inside. His only word to the operator was "ambulance." As sirens wailed in the distant background, Terrence got into his car across the street, and drove away into the night.

Epilogue

"Four Days have passed with no clues in the MegaSaver Massacre. Good evening, I'm Arnold Knight."

Leonard turned the television off and set the remote control on the side table next to his recliner. After several days of news reports and phone calls, Leonard was sick of hearing about the tragedy. He had even had to turn away a reporter from his door just this morning.

Leonard shook his head as he thought about poor Maxine. Before leaving the hospital, he had stopped by her room to say hello. Tubes ran into her throat from the machines behind her; wires ran from her chest to the electrical box next to her. An IV line stuck out from Maxine's wrist and stretched upward to the bag of fluids and medicine on her other side. Her eyes were closed; the silence of the room was occasionally broken by the pulse of the heart monitor and the oxygen being artificially pumped into her lungs. With nothing he could do for her, Leonard said his goodbyes to her door and took a taxi cab home.

Leonard's eyes now fell to the large stack of mail that had greeted him when he had arrived. He'd been putting it off for days, trying to enjoy his newfound health. His chest was loose again, and his breath flowed easily. His knee was still a little sore, but it would heal in time. He was even feeling steadier on his feet thanks to the cholesterol and diabetes medication he was on. The only problems that Leonard now faced were financial ones.

With the store's closing, and his extended hospital stay, Leonard was facing a huge monetary deficit. Insurance and social security would take care of a large chunk of the bills, but he would still be left with an insurmountable sum to contend with. He rubbed his hands together as he thought of the unpaid funeral expenses he had gone back to work to pay off in the first place. What could he do about that now? With all of his health problems, and notoriety associated with the "MegaSave Massacre", he wondered if he could get another job.

Leonard sorted through his stack of bills and junk mail, tossing the unimportant papers to the side and opening the others. As he finally reached that day's mail, a letter from the hospital caught Leonard's attention. He opened it cautiously, expecting the breath to be knocked out of him by the amount owed. To his astonishment, the total was zero.

Chalking it up to a mistake, Leonard set the bill to the side and opened an envelope from the funeral home that handled his wife's burial. Once again, he found he owed nothing. Half an hour, and several phone calls later, Leonard found that neither statement was in error. The hospital debt he had feared, and the funeral expenses he had gone back to work for, had all vanished. Someone out there had erased them all.

Leonard dropped the papers and walked over to the fireplace mantel. He picked up his favorite picture of Gladys and held it to his heart. It had been such a strange few weeks. So many people had been killed or harmed, himself included. None of that mattered to him any longer. He could now spend his life with his memories in the home he had shared with his wife. Leonard clutched his wife's photo to his chest and wept tears of joy.